Midnight Angel

Betsy St. Amant

I0663197

Midnight Angel
COPYRIGHT 2006, 2016 by Betsy Ann St. Amant

All scripture quotations, unless otherwise indicated, are taken from the Holy Bible, New International Version(R), NIV(R), Copyright 1973, 1978, 1984, 2011 by Biblica, Inc.™ Used by permission of Zondervan. All rights reserved worldwide. www.zondervan.com

Cover Art by *Nicola Martinez*

White Rose Publishing, a division of Pelican Ventures, LLC
www.pelicanbookgroup.com PO Box 1738 *Aztec, NM * 87410

White Rose Publishing Circle and Rosebud logo is a trademark of Pelican Ventures, LLC

Publishing History
First White Rose Edition, 2006 (The Wild Rose Press, Inc)
Second White Rose Edition, 2016
Paperback Edition ISBN 978-1-61116-909-6
Electronic Edition ISBN 978-1-61116-910-2
Published in the United States of America

Dedication

To the Author and Finisher of my faith, Jesus Christ.
Without Him, my words are in vain.

To Rebecca, the girl with the golden ticket. Thanks for
giving me that first boost!

To my family, especially Marie Raney. Thanks for
being my biggest fans!

To Lori Chally, for your encouraging friendship (and
peanuts!)

To the "real" Shan—thanks for calling me Author when
this was all still a dream.

To all my friends in the ACFW—too many to name,
but each of you hold a special place in my heart!

Prologue

Madison Lawrence tilted her face toward the inky starlit sky, closed her eyes and breathed in the chilly air. The night held a mysterious quality; she could feel it in her bones. A restless feeling resided deep inside her, reaching upward as if trying to grasp the stars above. She could sense it. This night had the potential to be magical.

She wrapped her fur coat tighter against her slender body. The wind picked up, carrying on its tail a bitterness that seeped deep within, but she was so distracted she barely noticed.

"I can't take it anymore." Madison heaved a sigh and watched her breath form a cloud that floated into the night. The cheerful sounds of the adults inside the museum behind her carried through the window. She was so tired of the parties. This was supposed to be a family trip, but her father, as always, had mixed business with pleasure. He was inside the ornate building now, probably making another toast to riches and fame. Madison blinked back tears, not sure if they were from the cold wind or the emotions boiling beneath the surface of her heart.

She sniffed, still able to smell the remnants of spicy cinnamon and eggnog clinging to her garments. She had to get fresh air. Darting a quick glance left and right down the deserted city street, she decided it would be safe to walk just a few blocks. The streets were brightly lit; the lamps lining the roadside radiated miniature halos that blurred through her teary eyes.

She began to walk. "I just want to be free," she whispered, "Free from the questions, and the stares, and the reputation of being Teddy Lawrence's daughter." Madison loved her father, but sometimes, enough was enough. And tonight, she'd definitely had enough. In all her eighteen years, she couldn't remember ever disliking her dad this much. She kept walking.

Finally looking up from her stroll, Madison paused long enough to gain her bearings. She had been in Germany for almost three weeks, but she didn't remember ever coming to this part of the city before. She thought she had been heading toward the city square, a tourist spot she had visited numerous times over the past several days. She must have taken a wrong turn, for she now stood before a giant, elegantly carved clock tower and a beautiful display of fountains. Despite the cold temperature, different levels of water splashed joyfully into the frigid air. She thought she recognized the garden across the street, but she wasn't sure.

"You shouldn't be out alone this time of night, *fraulein*."

Startled, Madison spun to see a young man slowly approaching. He couldn't have been more than a few years older than she, but Madison tensed, ready to run if necessary. Surprisingly, something about his easy demeanor didn't scare her. She relaxed.

Hands resting casually in his jacket pockets, the

man walked closer until he was standing right in front of her. She lifted her chin.

"Or perhaps angels have no fear." He grinned and something in Madison's heart jumped.

"No name, either?" The mysterious stranger asked with a strong German accent. His eyes sparkled with amusement, even in the dim light of evening.

"It's Madison," she responded. "Madison Lawrence." She wondered if the name would register with him. She half hoped it wouldn't. He was handsome. Mysterious. Alluring. Broad and muscular, he stood several inches taller than Madison. Hair the perfect mixture of blond and brown covered his head in a windblown sweep that brought attention to his startling clear blue eyes. Whiskered stubble covered his lower jaw, giving him a rugged, outdoor look that was far different from the perfectly groomed dates that often swarmed Madison's door.

"Madison Lawrence," the man repeatedly slowly, drawing out each syllable as if the words tasted sweet. He ducked down and looked closely at her face. "Of the Lawrence Industries in the United States? The Lawrence Towers? The Lawrence National Bank?"

"The very same," Madison admitted between clenched teeth. She mentally kicked herself. She should have kept her name a secret. Would she ever learn?

"Well, Madison. I can see that name has left a bitter taste in your mouth. We can't have that." He walked in a slow circle around her, studying her closely. "I shall have to call you Maddie."

Madison's heart leapt at the sound of a nickname coming from this man. Who was he? Lifting her chin, Madison looked into his disarming grin. "And what might I call you?"

"Prince Charming will work fine," he responded without hesitation. He leaned back on his heels and studied Madison seriously. Then he asked the last thing she expected. "Would you like to dance?"

Madison quickly glanced around the deserted courtyard. "Dance? Here? Now?"

"*Ja, tanzen.* Dance." He easily hopped onto the little wall surrounding the fountains and held out his hand.

Everything in Madison's head told her this was ridiculous, that she shouldn't be out with a stranger this time of night, or ever, really. She had no clue who this man truly was or even his name.

"There's no music," she protested, as if that were her biggest hesitation. She wiped her palms down the sides of her fur coat then regretted the action. Her mother would have a fit. Madison took a deep breath. Why did it suddenly feel as though the temperature had risen fifty degrees? She blinked. It was beginning to snow.

"Give me your hand," he coaxed.

And for some reason, she did.

Pulling her carefully onto the wall, he placed one hand lightly on her waist and held her other firmly in his.

"Just feel it," he whispered, beginning to sway back and forth. Madison, almost against her will, found herself moving with him, swaying to and fro on the fountain wall with her very own fairytale prince.

He began to hum softly, a nameless tune that brought strange comfort to Madison's heart. She closed her eyes and moved closer, enjoying the feel of his strong arm under her hand and the soft tendrils of hair that curled over the nape of his neck. Her gut screamed at her that this was crazy, complete and utter nonsense. Her parents would be livid. She knew better than this. But her heart had long since told her to be quiet.

Time seemed to stand still. They continued to dance on the wall, twirling, swaying, and moving to music only they could hear, in a rhythm only they could feel.

The hem of Madison's red party dress fluttered in the breeze, and her hair lifted in the wind.

"Like a halo," he whispered. "You really are an angel, Maddie." Catching her waist, the handsome German brought their dancing to an end and gently cupped her face with his free hand.

Madison's breath caught in her throat at the nearness of him, this stranger with whom she felt such an instant connection. She blinked, and snow fluttered off her eyelashes. This was absurd. Was he going to kiss her?

His gaze locked with hers, then trailed down her face to her lips, then back to her eyes. Warmth draped Madison's body until she no longer felt the cold night air. She stared back, unable and, at the same time, unwilling to break the connection. Leaning closer, he brushed his lips lightly against hers, so softly that Madison wasn't even sure it had happened.

"Maddie," he whispered against her lips. his warm breath sent chill bumps racing down her spine. *"Mein engel."*

He kissed her again, and this time Madison was sure. The touch of his lips against hers brought such a feeling of completeness, Madison was certain a part of her would be missing once they broke away. He lowered his head, kissing her more deeply, and Madison cupped her hands around the back of his neck. An hour passed, or possibly a minute. She wasn't sure. But none of it mattered—not her parent's inevitable reaction and panic, not her own absence of common sense. Nothing else existed. Just her and her mysterious prince.

Chiming from the clock tower sounded across the courtyard, and she broke away, gasping for breath and more than a little dizzy. "What time is it?" She gasped again and stared at the clock tower unable to comprehend what the pointing hands meant. Her head spun.

"Midnight," he said, loosening his hold on her waist but not completely letting go.

"I have to get back." Madison ran her hands briskly through her hair, feeling as if she had just been through a time warp. Was this a dream? How long had she been gone? Her parents would be wild with worry. But then, she didn't really care, did she?

"Will mein engel turn into a pumpkin?" Her mysterious stranger teased. He leaned forward and rested his forehead against hers.

Madison fought the instinct to stay in his arms and carefully stepped off the fountain wall instead.

He remained on the wall, hands in his pockets, watching her as she stumbled over her own heel and then caught her balance. "You don't understand," she explained desperately, walking backwards and nearly stumbling again. "My parents, they—"

He cut her off with a simple nod of his head, but didn't move from his sentry on the wall. Watching with what Madison thought to be the most gorgeous, clear eyes she'd ever seen, he gave her a smile that made her legs go weak. "I understand, sweet princess. The ball does not last forever."

Madison hesitated, considering her options. She could stay at the fountain with this handsome stranger, or she could do her duty as a daughter and heir and return to the party with her parents. Her heart twisted and shouted an instinct that Madison quickly rejected. "I'm sorry," she replied, still backing away one step at a time. "I have to go." She wished her heart didn't hurt so badly at the thought.

She turned and walked faster.

"Carsten!" he shouted.

She froze and then slowly turned around.

"My name is Carsten." He repeated, softly this time.

Madison rolled the name around in her head, loving it more with each second that passed. Carsten. Her very own German prince, Carsten.

"Carsten," she whispered out loud. The corners of her lips turned upwards in a smile that she couldn't contain. "Carsten."

"We shall meet again, my angel," he called out. Madison lifted her hand in a wave, and then held it closely over her heart as she turned and walked three more steps away.

Risking a glance over her shoulder, Madison blinked.

He was gone.

1

Six years later...

Madison threw her pen onto her desk in frustration. The design in front of her still didn't look right. Tilting her head, she studied the paper with a practiced eye. Something about the arrangement of the furniture...there was no harmony in the room.

She pressed the intercom button on the phone with a manicured nail. "Shan! I need you!" Releasing the button, she tapped her foot under the desk.

"You rang?" Madison's partner and best friend, Shan Rimmer, stepped into the luxury office, sarcastic as usual.

"This design isn't working. I need your eye."

Shan sauntered around to Madison's side of the desk and leaned over the drawing. Her dark hair spilled over her shoulder. "The angles, maybe?"

While Shan studied the paper, Madison leaned back in her chair and blew at a stray strand that had fallen from her clip. After graduating from New York State with a degree in interior design, Madison had started her own business with a little help from Daddy's Bank Account. The fact that it was a success wasn't surprising, for Madison spent every waking moment in the office or working off the clock. She had built an impressive clientele within the last year and had decorated everything from her cousin's nursery to the mayor's dining room. Having spent the majority of her life on her parent's plantation home in Georgia, Madison prided herself on being able to give her clients a "little taste of the South".

"You should definitely rearrange the furniture." Shan picked up a pencil from the cup on Madison's desk. Quickly sketching a few lines that indicated which pieces to swap, she dropped the pencil back on the desk with a dramatic flair. "There!"

"You're a genius, my friend." Madison eyed the much-improved design.

"I know." Shan twirled a strand of long hair around her finger and struck a pose beside Madison's desk. "I'm the Queen."

"Of drama," Madison teased. She stuck her tongue out and rolled backwards in her chair. She lifted her arms in a stretch and kicked off her high-heeled shoes to enjoy a moment of relief. With this design almost complete, she could take a quick break. Maybe even go home early, after her last appointment for the day.

And do…what? Madison's shoulders dropped as she contemplated her lack of options. Her job was her life, and her only friend was her partner. A smile tipped the corners of Madison's mouth as she remembered the graduation ceremony from the prestigious design school they had both attended.

"Hey, Madison. I've heard about the business you're planning to open."

Madison had turned and seen Shan approaching, hands on hips. She had smiled at her fun-loving, feisty friend. "That's right. Madison's

Designs. I plan on opening in a few weeks. The paperwork is already under way."

Shan tossed her head in her usual diva fashion. "Well, if you change the name to M & S Designs, then you should have no problem letting me be your partner."

Madison quirked an eyebrow. "And why would I do that?" It didn't sound like a bad idea, but she couldn't let Shan call the shots this early in the game.

Shan grinned. "Because I'm the best, and you know it."

Madison couldn't help but laugh. "Well I don't know about that name you suggested, but let's get some coffee and talk." In the end, Shan had gotten her way, and they became a top team in the city.

Though they were about as opposite as they can get. Back in the present, Madison grinned as she took in the sight of her friend standing by the bookshelves that lined the office walls. Madison, tall, slender, and blonde, was a complete workaholic with a drive for perfectionism, while Shan's easy-going, fun-loving personality complemented her wavy dark tresses and skin the color of rich cocoa. They were opposites, but they were the perfect team.

"Girl, I'm gonna ask one more time. What is the deal with the angel collection?" Shan waved her arm dramatically in the general direction of the bookshelves. Madison rolled her eyes and slipped her feet back into her pumps. "It's just a thing," she insisted. "I wouldn't call it a collection. There's not that many."

Then, just like it always did when someone mentioned angels, her mind raced back to that enchanted evening several years ago. Closing her eyes, Madison entered her favorite time warp and could almost sense the snow on her face, the feel of a certain German's arms around her and…

"Delivery for Ms. Lawrence."

A deep voice jerked Madison out of her reverie, and she slid down in her desk chair, losing her shoe.

Her regular route UPS man, Tony, stood standing in her doorway with a smirk, clutching a package wrapped in brown paper. "The shipping address is for your home, but I knew you'd be here and would want it right away. The boss said he'd make an exception this once. You are a preferred customer, after all." He set the box on the desk and held out the electronic clipboard. "Sign here."

Righting herself in her chair with as much dignity as she could muster, Madison scrawled her signature on the tiny screen. "Thanks, Tony." She handed back the form and waited until he left the office before grabbing for the box.

Shan was faster. "What do we have here?" She held the box out of Madison's reach. Cutting open the flaps, she dove into the package.

"Aha!"

"What?" Madison questioned with pretend innocence, since she already knew.

"Not really a collection, you said?" Shan grinned as she pulled an antique porcelain angel out of the box and fluffed its' feathery wings.

Feeling a blush creep up her face, Madison bolted from her chair and grabbed for the doll. She reached to put it in place on the nearest shelf, behind a row of smaller angels. "It's nothing," she insisted. She smoothed the wings back into shape and adjusted its position on the shelf. This one was truly beautiful. The angel's delicate face was hand-painted, and her gown a deep velvety red—the same shade that reminded her of the dress she'd worn the night she danced with Carsten. But how could she possibly explain to Shan something that made no sense even to herself? How could she say that for some unexplainable reason, each time she bought an angel, she felt a little bit closer to her very own fairytale prince?

"One day, I'm gonna learn about this secret you're hiding." Shan crossed her arms over her business suit and shook her head in mock pity. "You're not the collectibles type, Madison. And you definitely don't do things without a reason."

"I never said I didn't have a reason," Madison said softly.

"What was that?" Shan raised an eyebrow.

"I said, let's go grab a latte. I'm parched." She grabbed her designer purse and ushered her nosy partner out of her office.

"I can take a hint," Shan retorted as she locked the door. "Hey, aren't we important enough yet to have someone bring us the lattes?"

~*~

Madison stared out the window of the taxi; absently tapping her finger against the lid of her half-empty cup. A prayer rose within. "Lord, what is with these random flashbacks? Shan mentions my angel collection and it's like my mind can't think of anything but that night." She prayed silently as she continued to gaze at the passing scenery of buildings after buildings. The nearest coffee shop was only a few blocks away from her office complex, but Shan had insisted that she didn't want to walk in her new high heels. Now, because of the traffic, the taxi ride back was taking forever.

"Get out of the way, you crazy—" The cab driver shook his fist out the open window as he let loose a string of expletives. Madison cringed. Shan giggled.

"I just love New York," Shan commented, stirring her coffee in little circles as she talked. "I couldn't live without the big city bustle! The people, the drama, the action… I love it!"

Madison bit her lip. *The pollution, the crazy drivers, the lack of grass or anything green, for that matter*…It was springtime in New York, but it was hard to tell aside from the weather. Unless one walked uptown to Central Park, it was difficult to find flowers or much greenery. But who had time for those indulgences? There was work to be done, always work to be done.

She stared down at the lid of her coffee cup and thought wistfully of the lush acreage at home in Georgia. The plantation was always so beautiful this time of year, from the azaleas blooming outside her bedroom window to the clumps of honeysuckle covering the fences. Sometimes Madison doubted her decision to move to New York, but she knew her design business would never take off in Georgia. Maybe if she made a big enough name for herself, she could relocate and still keep her clientele. It was a thought she frequently entertained. However, there was the down side that came with spending too much time with her father. Ever since her mother had been killed in a car accident five years ago, her dad had become incredibly overprotective.

Her stomach twisted as she remembered the past years of being told what to wear, whom to date, where to go... Her natural being was far more independent than that. She shook her head, forcing away the bad memories.

Ignoring Shan's ramblings about how fabulous city life was, Madison once again looked out her window and into the passenger side of another taxi. A man about her age sat perched on the backseat, leaning forward and drumming his fists in an impatient rhythm against the front seat. It looked as if he was as desperate to escape his taxi as she. Madison smiled in amusement, thinking that at least she wasn't the only one with a lack of love for the city traffic.

The man turned and glanced out the window right back at Madison. Madison blushed, embarrassed to be caught staring, and quickly ducked her head. Suddenly, she jerked her gaze back to the window and her eyes widened in shock. No. It couldn't be. He had the same hair color, sure, and the cut was similar, but there was no way. What were the odds? Silly girl, Madison scolded herself. It'd been six years. She wasn't remembering correctly.

She dared to glance once more as her taxi began to pull away. This time, her gaze locked with his and in a heartbeat, she knew. No one else had eyes that color, eyes that reminded her heart of a clear winter sky in Germany. No one but him.

2

"Crazy," Madison mumbled as she banged her head repeatedly against her desktop. "I'm going crazy. No, I've gone crazy."

"Maddie!" Shan burst into Madison's office. "What are you doing to the desk?"

Madison's head snapped up. "What did you just say?" She hadn't heard that nickname since it had come from Carsten's lips six years ago.

Shan slowly backed away from Madison. "I think I called you Maddie. Is that bad?"

"You've never called me that before," Madison replied. She stood up and put her hands on her hips.

Shan threw her hands in the air in a sign of surrender. "It just slipped out. I don't know why, I'm not exactly accustomed to seeing you assault your desk. I probably wasn't thinking clearly."

Madison rubbed her pounding temples and sank back into her desk chair. "Never mind," she muttered. "I'm sorry, Shan. I guess I've had too much caffeine today." She watched as her friend slipped quickly out of the office. Madison knew what had her emotions all stirred up but refused to admit it.

Madison executed a slow spin in her chair, desperate for clarity. "There is no possible way that the man in the taxi was Carsten." She spoke the words slowly and deliberately. Maybe the more times she said it; the sooner she'd believe it.

~*~

Madison straightened in her chair. It was almost time for her four o'clock appointment, and she didn't want her new client to think she was crazy.

She reached into the desk drawer for her client's file. "Mr. Erlichman," she read out loud, as she shuffled through the papers. "Interested in price quotes and design ideas for an inherited estate." Madison had never decorated an entire house before, just individual rooms. This had the potential to be a very profitable job. Her spirits lifted. "Lord, I could really use this sale. Give me wisdom, please."

The speaker on her phone buzzed, and Shan's voice filled the room. "Ms. Lawrence, your four o'clock is here," she murmured in her professional voice. Madison bit back a grin and shook her head. Their receptionist had quit earlier in the week. Shan had volunteered to play secretary until they found a replacement, stating that "it would be fun". Better Shan than Madison, in Madison's opinion.

"Send him in." Madison rose to meet her new, and apparently wealthy, client. Satisfied that she projected the image of a professional, yet approachable designer, Madison trained a smile on the door and smoothed the front of her tailored jacket over her pencil skirt.

The frosted glass door swung open. Shock overtook her and all thoughts of professionalism flew from Madison's head. Her smile transformed into a gaping mouth.

"You!" she gasped.

The handsome German in her doorway

responded only with a smile.

Madison's legs went weak.

She gulped.

The room spun.

She collapsed to the floor.

~*~

"Is she all right?" Shan whispered.

"I think she hit her head." The male voice held concern.

"No, that bump was already there."

"Why?"

"She beat up her desk."

"She did what?" The concern turned to confusion.

Madison forced open her eyes. She pulled herself to a sitting position, ignoring the pounding in her head. She tried to focus on the two people crouched beside her on the floor. Shan's image swam into view along with a male figure that made Madison feel certain she was in a dream.

"Wake up," she commanded herself out loud. "Wake up! Right now."

"Oh, no, she's gone cuckoo." Shan tilted her head and spoke loudly to Madison, as if the increase in volume would make a difference. "You are awake, Partner."

A masculine chuckle sounded from Madison's right and for the first time, she looked closely at the man who had entered her office and caused this whole commotion.

"You really know how to make a guy feel *willkommen*—welcome," he joked.

"Carsten?" Madison whispered. "But how? Why

did—I don't understand."

"That makes two of us," Shan responded, gaze moving from Madison to Mr. Erlichman and back again. "Who's Carsten?"

Madison realized she was still sitting on the ground and struggled to rise. Carsten's arm shot out to steady her, and when his fingers touched her hand, it felt as if her entire arm burst into flame.

Shan's eyebrows rose. "Do you two know each other?"

Madison glared at her partner. "Do I hear the phone ringing?"

Shan shook her head innocently. Madison's eyes narrowed further.

"Oh, that phone." Shan shot Madison a look that said you had better explain this later and then left the room.

Madison took a deep breath to steady herself and attempted to twist her skirt back into its proper position on her hips. She briefly wondered if she had flashed anyone during her collapse, then realized it didn't really matter. This situation couldn't get any more embarrassing than it already was.

Daring to glance up, she caught Carsten watching her with a steady gaze, and felt flustered once again. Why wasn't he saying anything?

"Maybe we should start over," she began, trying desperately to put some edge of professionalism back into her voice. "I'm sorry about fainting. I don't think I ate enough lunch today. We've been awfully busy. Perhaps you'd like a cup of coffee? Starbucks it's not, but it's hot, at least." She rambled on, and with a sweep of her arm, motioned to the coffee system on the counter across the room. In doing so, she slammed her knuckles into the sharp corner of her desk.

"Oh!" Madison stuffed her scraped fingers into her mouth.

Carsten reached out and assisted Madison into her desk chair.

"There now," he said," Let me see your hand." Madison, rendered helpless just by the sound of his voice, surrendered her knuckles to his inspection.

"Just a scrape," Carsten announced after a brief check of her hand. He gently raised her hand to his mouth and brushed his lips across her injury. "All better," he whispered, not dropping her gaze.

Madison snatched her hand back as if it were on fire, certain her heart would at any moment beat right out of her chest and go bouncing across her office.

"Perhaps we should begin discussing your business," Madison stated, pretending she still couldn't feel the imprint of his lips on her knuckles. She motioned for Carsten to take the chair on the other side of the desk.

Obediently, he dropped into the suggested leather seat and smiled. "Business, you say?"

"Yes. Business. You're here for a reason, I presume?" Other than giving her a stroke at age twenty-five, of course.

"Still in a hurry, aren't you Maddie?" Carsten responded, his eyes gleaming with something indefinable. "I suppose some things never change, no matter how much time or distance has been spent."

Madison mentally caught her jaw before it

dropped, and squared her shoulders. "I'll have you know that I happen to take plenty of time for myself, thank you very much. As if it's any of your business."

Carsten's eyebrows rose and he leaned forward, elbows braced on his knees, to look her straight in the eyes. "What's your favorite television program?"

Madison's mouth went dry and her mind raced to think of the name of a current series or sitcom, any show at all. But she had none, because she never watched TV. She worked nonstop. *How does he know this much about me?*

"That's what I thought." He settled back into the chair.

Madison closed her eyes briefly, determined to compose herself and regain the upper hand in the conversation. *How can you regain what you never had, Madison?* Her eyes flew open and she decided to concentrate on the file in front of her.

"Your file mentions you have inherited an estate. That's very interesting. Where is it located? How many square feet?" Madison went through the checklist questions like clockwork, having done so hundreds of times with other clients. She doodled on the edge of the page, hoping she appeared to be taking notes instead of reeling with shock.

"Montana."

Madison's head jerked up. She stared at Carsten in disbelief. "I'm sorry, I thought you said Montana."

"Big Sky Country, so I hear," Carsten replied with a grin. "When do we leave?"

3

Madison wasn't sure how much time passed as she sat in her desk chair with her mouth hanging open like a five-year-old seeing FAO Schwartz for the first time. What had just happened? The morning had started off normal enough. Never in her wildest imagination had Madison ever pictured the very star of her midnight dreams waltzing back into her life as casually as she strolled in to Starbucks every morning.

She stared at Carsten across the desk. How did this man make time seem to stop? Madison remembered a snowy night not so long ago when the world ceased to spin and everything in the universe held its breath as an unlikely couple shared a heart bonding kiss...Madison's cheeks warmed at the memory and she cleared her throat, snapping back into reality. *Get it together, girl. That was a long time ago. Be professional!*

Reality, however, remained a bit cloudy, for the very object of her dreams was still sitting in his chair, now chewing a piece of gum as if he wasn't a part of her personal life-altering catastrophe.

"Let me get this straight." Madison cleared her throat. "You're asking me to leave New York and go to Montana with you to decorate your ranch house?"

Carsten nodded as though there were no reason

at all for her to be so dramatic.

"How did a German like yourself inherit a ranch in the States, anyway?" Madison drummed her pencil in an impatient rhythm against the file folder on her desk.

"A close friend of the family just passed on, and I have decided to make it my home away from home while I am in America." Carsten smiled warmly and Madison's stomach did a flip.

"Do you do a lot of business in the U.S.?"

"Some."

"Whereabouts?"

"Here and there."

Madison furrowed her brow and wondered why she rarely got a straight answer from him.

"So, I ask again, when can we get started?" Carsten scooted forward in his chair and leaned eagerly toward Madison.

He winked, and Madison tried desperately to remember all the reasons why she couldn't run off to Montana with this man.

"I don't know how things work in Germany, but I can't just take off across the country without notice." Madison found it was much easier to talk while avoiding eye contact, so she again glanced down at the file on her desk. She shuffled some pages.

Carsten waited in silence.

Fighting a blush, Madison added. "Plus, it wouldn't be proper for me to stay there with you alone. Assuming, of course, there is no Mrs. Erlichman?" Her voice trailed off.

Carsten propped his chin on his fingers. "No wife. I have staff there. We would not be alone."

"Women staff, included?" Madison held her breath. She told herself that knowing this could be a deciding factor, if indeed she lost her sanity and agreed to go, but even she heard a hint of jealousy in her tone as she tried to ignore the fact that his declaration of bachelorhood had sent her heart into an erratic rhythm. How had he remained single? Were all the women in Germany blind?

"Certainly. The ranch is run by a dear friend of my father's. If I remember correctly, her cooking is *sehr gut*." Carsten smiled.

Madison gulped and tried to think of another obstacle. She knew she could leave the business for a few weeks. Shan was more than capable of taking care of their pickier clients, and the rest could wait until she returned. This would, of course, bring in a great paycheck... Madison blinked as she realized how close she was to traipsing off across the country with a man she had met once in what might as well have been a dream.

At least his sudden reappearance confirmed that the night long ago had, indeed, happened. Some days, she'd not been entirely sure.

Her cellphone rang, a sharp interruption to her run-away thoughts. She glanced at the number, and didn't recognize it. "Excuse me." She turned sideways in her chair and flipped open the phone. "This is Madison."

"Hello. I'm calling in regards to the angel you recently purchased online."

Madison sat up straighter. "Yes, I received the package today. The delivery was very prompt. I appreciate that." She glanced at Carsten, who was watching her with a grin. She looked away.

"You don't understand. I need the angel back." The tone darkened.

Madison frowned. Who did this guy think he was? "I'm sorry, but the sale was final. I've already grown quite attached to the angel. I have a collection."

"I understand that, miss, but the problem is that I sold it by accident. My brother will be very upset if he does not get it back. It's of extreme value to him—a family heirloom of sorts." He was talking faster now, sounding almost desperate.

With a sigh, Madison touched her fingers to the sides of her pounding head. She couldn't take this right now. She had to deal with Carsten first.

"I'm very sorry, but I can't help you. Thank you for calling." Madison shut the phone with a quick motion, confused that someone would try to reverse the sale. In all her many transactions, she had never had such a request.

"Sorry about the interruption." Madison shoved her phone back into her purse and folded her hands in her lap, mostly to keep them from shaking.

"All is fine. So, we were just discussing when you might be able to start the project." Carsten's eyes warmed and Madison felt like diving right into them. She fought the instinct and stood abruptly.

"Carsten, I can't go," she blurted before she could change her mind. She held out her hand for a professional, polite handshake. "Thank you for the generous offer, but I can't leave my business at this time."

He needed to leave, now. Her stilted tone and formal language wouldn't hide her heart for long.

Carsten rose slowly from his seat and accepted

the handshake, never breaking eye contact. "As you wish, mein engel." With a nod and without a glance back, he once again disappeared from her life.

As before, time froze in place. Madison sat and stared at the empty chair across from her, wondered how it was possible that one man could leave such a strong presence behind while taking her heart along with him. It didn't seem to be a very fair trade.

Carsten's words echoed in her ears. "My angel," he had called her. Not sure how long she sat staring at an empty space that used to hold a miracle, Madison jumped when Shan appeared in the open doorway.

"Please tell me you did not send that handsome man packin'."

Madison dropped her head onto her folded arms and mumbled against the desktop. "I did."

"Madison," Shan whined, drawing out her friend's name until it sounded six syllables long. She dropped into the chair that Carsten had vacated and crossed her arms over her chest. "Are you nuts? The finest looking man I've ever seen waltzes in here and offers to sweep you off your feet, and you all but say 'no thanks, I like standing right here in my designer heels just fine'."

Madison raised her head just enough to look at Shan. "You were eavesdropping?"

Shan's gaze fell to the floor and she shifted in her chair. "Not eavesdropping, exactly. Just, you know...intentionally not turning off the intercom after I buzzed him in."

Madison groaned and let her head drop back against the desk. "You're right, I'm an idiot."

"I never said that," Shan argued.

"But it's true."

Madison was greeted with silence at her claim. It was true. She had just turned down a once-in-a-lifetime opportunity, and for what? The smog of New York City? The crazy cab drivers? The thirteen-hour workdays?

"You need a vacation," Shan stated.

Madison raised her head and watched as Shan grabbed Carsten's file from the desktop. She flipped through the pages until she found what she was looking for, made a quick notation, and then she slammed the file down beside Madison.

Circled in Shan's signature purple pen was Carsten's cellphone number.

"You know what to do." Shan gave an encouraging smile and slipped out the office.

"I'll even keep the intercom off for privacy," she hollered from the other room.

Madison grinned in spite of herself and absently traced the number with her thumbnail. One phone call and her life could change forever. She narrowed her gaze and envisioned a list of pros and cons, justifying the evidence of what she wanted Jetting off to Montana for a few weeks wasn't really all that more spontaneous or dangerous that dancing with Carsten on the wall in Germany. And that had turned out fine.

That is, if *fine* meant her heart had been on a roller coaster ever since.

She thumped her fist on the table, determined to quiet the multiple voices arguing in her head. "Do it, Madison. Make the call. This will be good for your career."

Madison picked up the phone, dialed all but the

last number and then slammed down the receiver. Who was she kidding? She could never be that daring. Not for her career. Not even for love.

4

Madison multitasked as she entered her apartment. She kicked off her shoes at the door and dropped her keys into the holder on the marble entry table, all while flipping through that day's mail and wondering what she had in the freezer to heat for dinner. Hopefully something other than another lasagna.

Throwing her discarded mail into a pile on the table, Madison rolled her neck to the side and then to the front in a stretch before turning to head down the hall. She stopped dead in her tracks, mouth open in shock. Heart pounding, Madison turned a slow circle, taking in her surroundings.

Her apartment had been ransacked. Drawers hung open, pillows and couch cushions lay in heaps on the floors, pictures had been knocked off the walls and chairs upturned. Madison clutched her hand against her chest and fought back a wave of panic, trying to steady the out-of-control rhythm of her heart. What had happened?

Common sense told her to get out of the apartment, but she couldn't move. Her feet stuck to the carpet as fear caught her breath in her throat. Madison stood frozen in place, afraid to breathe, listening for any sounds that would prove the intruder was still inside. Silence, other than the steady ticking of the kitchen clock and her own pulsing blood pounding a rhythm in her ears.

Madison peeked around the corner of the hall and into the kitchen, not sure what to expect. It, too, was upturned, though not as badly as the living area. Madison plucked a steak knife from the spilled silverware on the tile floor and then crept slowly down the hall. She'd check the bathroom first.

Holding her breath, Madison stepped into the room. Her bare feet were silent on the tile floor. The purple lacy shower curtain fluttered in the draft from the air conditioner vent above. Madison raised her knife, hoping she looked more intimidating than she felt. What would she do with the knife if she discovered someone behind the curtain? Horror stories of victims being killed with their own weapons swam in her head. *Oh, God...help me.* She grabbed the curtain and yanked.

Nothing.

Madison sagged against the wall and lowered her trembling hand. She sucked in air. She couldn't relax just yet. Still several rooms to go.

Wielding her knife, she flung open closet doors making noises that resembled a Tarzan yell. When she'd finally finished the once-over of her home, she collapsed in a pile of nerves on her bedroom floor.

She curled up in a ball and rested her chin on her knees. Her body shook uncontrollably. What was she going to do? How would she even begin to put her home back together? How did the intruder get in? What did he want? Was it some kind of sick joke? Madison's thoughts ran together in a confused jumble, and she finally decided the best plan was to call the police and then find out how her apartment had been broken into.

After making the call to 911, Madison walked about her apartment, checking every window. None seemed to have been bothered. She knew the front door had been locked when she came in, because she remembered struggling with the deadbolt. That left the back door and the fire escape as a possibility.

Madison held her breath as she approached the door that led out of her storage room and to the fire escape down the back of her apartment unit. Time seemed to stand still. Did she even want to look? Sweat beaded on her brow, and she tightened her grip on the doorknob. One, two, three...She ripped it open and held up the knife. The room was empty. But sure enough, the outside door to the stairs was not only busted open, it was half hanging off its hinges.

Icy fear crept its way down Madison's spine, tightening like a vice until she could barely breathe. The cruel image of someone kicking in her door and tearing apart her apartment left her gasping for air.

She let the knife slip from her limp fingers and crouched down, putting her head between her knees. She tried to breathe slowly and deeply, but the panic wouldn't fade. She coughed—almost choked—as the fear pressed in tighter. Madison forced her nerves to obey. "Breathe. Just breathe." She could get through this. It was just a robbery, right? She lived in New York City. She'd seen a lot of things. Heard a lot of things. She should be more rational than this.

A sudden pounding on her front door set the terror back into motion. Madison started. "Police!" came the brusque voice from the other side.

Madison peered through the peephole to see

two uniformed officers, a man and a woman, standing on her welcome mat. She ushered the pair inside. They introduced themselves as Officers Peterson and Wilburg.

"Looks like a definite ransack," Officer Peterson stated after a glimpse around the apartment. Madison barely refrained from rolling her eyes at his announcement of the obvious. She cleared her throat instead.

"Anything missing?" Officer Wilburg asked. She, at least, appeared sympathetic as she scribbled a few things on a notepad and looked at Madison with expectant eyes.

"I—I don't know." Madison stammered. "I just got home and found my apartment like this. I haven't really gone through anything." She decided to omit her earlier search of the apartment. There was no reason for these two officers to think her any dumber than she already felt. It'd been stupid, checking things out on her own.

Officer Wilburg raised an eyebrow and made another notation on her paper.

Madison tapped her foot, impatience and adrenaline brimming over. If she had called the cops sooner, would they have been able to do more? It wasn't as if she had tampered with the evidence. But what did she know about any of this, anyway?

Maybe she should have been watching some crime dramas on TV all these years, after all.

The cops dusted some items for fingerprints, but to no avail. Officer Wilburg turned to Madison and looked her straight in the eyes. Madison's heart stopped. By the look on Wilburg's face, this wasn't going to be good news. She took a deep breath.

"If you have someplace else to stay for a while, I'd suggest doing so. We don't have much to work with here. Hopefully something will turn up. Sometimes, things like this just happen, and nothing ever comes from it. Other times..." The officer's voice trailed off, and Madison caught the gist of what the woman wasn't saying. Other times, people got hurt. She swallowed hard and nodded.

After filling out the report and responding to several more questions she couldn't answer, Madison was almost relieved when the police left. They had, at least, helped her secure the back door, though to little effect. Madison knew she couldn't stay home alone that night. If someone had broken in once, they could break in again, just as the policewoman suggested. And then what would she do?

Staring out the window into the foreboding blackness of the night, Madison ran her hands up and down her arms, fighting back the permanent chill that seemed to have taken over her body. What if someone was out there right now, watching...waiting?

She abruptly dropped the blinds and drew the curtains, determined to remain in control. She was an adult. She could handle this.

Madison thought about calling her father, but this would be just another incident for him to lord over her. She was tired of their constant fights. He'd always possessed this intense need for control that was forever clashing with her own desire for freedom. This wouldn't help matters. She could call Shan, who could come over and help clean up the apartment, but Madison hated to ask her friend to get back out after having had such a long workday. She knew Shan would come in an instant, but even though she was scared, Madison didn't want company. She wanted to be alone with her doubts and insecurities and try to make sense of them all. Shan would be good for a laugh and cheering up, that much was certain, but Madison wanted answers. And she was determined to find them, even if that meant putting her entire home back together by herself for clues.

Grabbing the nearest couch cushion, Madison shoved it back into place and then bent to grab the next. She worked like a woman on a mission for hours, not even stopping to eat dinner. Surprisingly, nothing was seriously damaged or destroyed, except for a few plates and mugs that had shattered on the kitchen floor. Madison was grateful for that much. However, her gratitude paled in at the realization that she hadn't found even a hint of what her intruder had sought.

Madison fought back a wave of helplessness as she dropped onto the couch. Was she a random target? Just another victim of New York City crime? She chewed absently on her lower lip. Why ransack but not steal anything? It didn't make sense. Did someone have a personal vendetta against her? But who? And why? All she did was work. What could she have of value—that the thief apparently didn't find?

Madison closed her eyes. She had no other life, no chances to offend anyone. And her clients all seemed normal enough. There was no explanation, no easy answer. She needed a plan, a course of action, anything to distract herself from these crazy circumstances. Make that dangerous circumstances. She cast a worried glance at the locked apartment door. She couldn't stay a second longer. But where could she go if not to her father or Shan?

An idea dawned, an idea completely ridiculous and without merit. But it was all she had. Within minutes, Madison had packed a bag with a change of clothes and some necessities and hailed a cab back to her office.

She needed that phone number.

5

"Hey, Miss," the cab driver piped up, glancing at Madison in the rearview mirror. "You got a jealous boyfriend or somethin'?"

Madison frowned and leaned forward, unclear as to what the cabbie meant. "No." That was an understatement. As if she'd even been on a date in the last six months.

"That black SUV's been behind us ever since I picked you up at your apartment."

Madison's eyes grew round and she sank lower in the seat, heart pounding. Images of the latest NYC headline crimes flashed through her mind. She didn't want to be another statistic. Thinking she would surely throw up, Madison fought back panic and tried to breathe.

Suddenly, a shot echoed through the night. Madison jumped. A second shot followed. Madison's heart jammed into her throat. She squeezed her eyes closed and prepared for the worst. When nothing happened, she forced her eyes open and turned to look out the back window. A glimpse of the SUV bouncing out of control across the median confirmed that the front tires had blown.

Or been shot out?

Not certain if she had been rescued or if her situation had just taken a turn for the worse, Madison gasped to the cabbie. "Go! You can lose them. Turn left at the next block and then double back to the address I gave you."

Never before had going to work been this stressful. Madison's thought's traveled back to a little rhyme her late grandma used to quote on bad days. "When all your plans go awry and all you want to do is cry, trust in God; He'll see you through, He always knows just what to do."

Did He? She hoped somebody was in control. She and God had always possessed a fragile relationship. She asked for help when she needed it, and He provided. Madison didn't want to bother Him with irrelevant details. He was busy, and so was she. Kind of like her real father.

However, in times like this...

Madison gulped. The cab pulled to a screeching halt in front of the doors to her office suite. Subtle.

Madison grabbed her bag and hurried out of the taxi, tossing the driver a bigger tip than originally planned. She thanked him over her shoulder as she ran inside the complex.

Madison unlocked the door to the suite and burst into her private office. She slammed the door and locked it behind her. Should she shove a piece of furniture under the knob? She reached for the desk chair then stopped. This was silly. No one knew where she was.

She took a deep breath and then grabbed Carsten's file, which was still on her desk where she had left it earlier. At the time, she had felt that shelving it would only confirm the fact that her favorite memory was once again just that—a memory shut out of her reality.

She flipped through the pages until she found

Carsten's cell number, circled in Shan's purple ink. Then she grabbed the phone, punching in the number with shaky fingers. She waited. A glance at her watch confirmed the time. 9:30 p.m.

The German accent she had already come to adore picked up on the second ring. "*Hallo.*"

Madison froze. What should she say? She wasn't sure why she had called in the first place; it was an act of pure instinct. She just craved safety, and for some unknown reason, Carsten represented that for her. The thought crossed her mind that it should be her father who represented that, but it wasn't. It was Carsten.

Carsten cleared his throat. "Is anyone there?" His voice brimmed with impatience.

Madison realized she had been silent the whole time she was thinking of what to say. "Carsten, I'm scared," she quickly blurted out.

She instantly bit her lip and regretted the words. A blush burned at the base of her neck. Not exactly the strong image she wanted to portray.

But right now, she didn't feel strong. She closed her eyes, and her spirit fought to maintain hope that maybe Carsten could actually help her.

"*Mein engel*—is that you?"

Her breath caught in her throat at the nickname he had given her and she opened her eyes. "Yes, it's Madison."

"Maddie, what's wrong?" Carsten's concern came through the phone loud and clear, and Madison felt a warmth seep through her chilled bones. She had all but thrown him out on his foreign backside earlier that afternoon, and now here he was, with no hard feelings, no resentment, just concern.

"Maddie, are you all right? Talk to me!"

Madison jerked out of her reverie and stammered into the receiver. "I'm here, Carsten. I need...I don't know what I need. Someone broke into my apartment while I was at work today. I don't want to go back home. I can't stay there."

"And you chose to call me?"

Madison bit her lip and nodded, then realized he couldn't see her. *Get it together, Madison.*

"I feel safe with you," she whispered. This time, the usual regret didn't pound on her heart's door immediately after.

There was a long pause. "I'll be right there. I assume you are calling from your office?"

"Yes. I'm at work. I thought I could sleep here." Wait. Why would he assume she was at work? She frowned, sudden doubt tugging at the pit of her stomach. Did he know more than she did?

Maybe she shouldn't feel safe with him after all.

But this was Carsten. If he'd meant anything ill toward her, it would've been revealed before now. It would've been revealed that night when she was alone and vulnerable at the fountain in Germany.

"You don't need to be alone. I'll pick you up and we can get dinner and talk. Does that sound good?"

His voice melted away her concerns. Her stomach grumbled in response to the mention of food, and she realized she hadn't eaten a thing since her salad at lunchtime.

"It does. Thank you."

"Five minutes." The receiver clicked. Madison didn't know what kind of story she'd fallen into, but her prince was on his way to rescue her.

~*~

Madison and Carsten settled into a cozy back booth at her favorite diner and sipped hot coffee while deciding on which soup to order.

"Chicken noodle for me," Carsten decided when the waitress approached the table.

With a brisk nod and a scratch with a pencil on her pad of paper, the woman turned expectant and impatient eyes to Madison.

Madison absently chewed her lip as she debated her options. "Broccoli and cheese, please. With an extra piece of bread."

Carsten sent her an amused look while the waitress fairly snatched their menus and strode away to put in their orders. "Are all New York food service workers that friendly?"

Madison grinned in spite of her current circumstances and nodded. "Pretty close to it. You should visit my father's home in the South. Everyone is friendly there. It's almost as if it's a national rule."

Something strange flickered in Carsten's eyes so fast Madison thought that maybe she had just imagined it.

"And what of your mother?" he asked.

Madison lowered her gaze. "She's gone." Carsten's silence indicated he understood. An uncomfortable quiet stretched across the table between them. Clearing her throat, Madison poured another packet of sugar into her coffee and reached for a spoon, but Carsten interfered.

"Your hands, they're shaking." He picked up the spoon and stirred her coffee with ease. "I don't see the point, personally. Coffee is only coffee when prepared strong and black." He winked at her and relinquished the mug.

"Then you, sir, will never be a true New Yorker." Relieved that the subject had been changed, Madison sipped her drink and closed her eyes, relishing the flavor almost as much as she relished Carsten's accent.

"I should hope not. Germany is my home."

"You're not going to stand on the table and sing your anthem, are you?" Madison suddenly felt more relaxed then she had in weeks. She returned his wink with one of her own. "You don't want to take me on in a singing contest."

"Ah, so you are an excellent singer, I presume?" Carsten reached for his own mug of coffee, which Madison noted was indeed, strong and black.

"Quite the contrary. I so much as hum under my breath and my business partner goes running for the stereo. She says even New York talk radio is better than listening to me."

Carsten chuckled, a warm sound that wrapped around Madison like a familiar quilt. "Shan seems like quite the character."

"She definitely keeps things interesting," Madison agreed.

The next few moments were spent in companionable silence, each sipping their warm broth. There didn't seem to be a problem in the world too big to solve with Carsten at her side. That realization frightened Madison almost more than the thought that someone was chasing her.

Shaking her head to clear it, Madison put down her spoon.

"You really are upset about this, aren't you?" Carsten asked.

Madison blew out a sharp breath and gave a short laugh, void of humor. "These types of things don't usually happen in my world."

"And what world is that?"

The question came so quickly that Madison had to pause to formulate her response. How much should she reveal? He was technically still a stranger. She looked up at him through lowered lids. A handsome stranger, but a stranger, nonetheless.

She hesitated before answering. "A safe world; a world of comfort and security and money at my disposal."

But was that world as safe as she assumed? Maybe she was being targeted *because* of her rich father.

That didn't explain the ransacking though—and the fact that nothing expensive had been stolen from her apartment. None of this made sense.

Carsten's eyes indicated she should continue, and she forced her mind back on track.

"I tried hard not to become the stereotypical 'spoiled little rich girl' but I never wanted for a thing. Except, of course, my father's undivided attention." That was an understatement. Teddy Lawrence assumed he could buy his daughter's affection with an unlimited credit card. She wanted his time and energy, not oversized teddy bears and designer clothes.

Carsten nodded, as if soaking in her words was the only pressing matter he had to attend to that night. Madison relished his attentiveness, and realized that if she wasn't careful, she could wind up pouring out her entire heart within the next few minutes.

"You need to come to Montana with me." His words sounded like a command, but his tone was pleading. "You'll be safe there. No fears. No worries."

Madison considered the idea once again, realizing that this opportunity was being presented to her for the second time in one day. Was that a sign? Was God urging her to go by reopening the door she had all but slammed shut? She shuddered, remembering the night's events. She did not want to return to her apartment alone. What other options did she have?

"I could go with you to your apartment while you packed," Carsten offered, almost as if he were reading her mind. He waited silently, eyebrows raised, waiting for her cue.

Did she trust him? Alone with her, in her apartment after it had been ransacked and she had been followed? A dozen reasons why she should say no raced through Madison's mind, but before she could even begin to sort through them, she felt herself nodding and saying, "OK. Let's go."

Carsten smiled and signaled the waitress for their bill. "You'll love Montana," he promised. "You need to escape. And I need you."

Madison's heart skipped a beat. He needed her? He'd not been exactly subtle with her before, what with the kiss at the fountain six years ago and the brush of his lips against her injured fingers in her office earlier. But this was outright bold.

She swallowed hard. "You—you do?"

"Of course." He pulled out his wallet for his

credit card. "The house is a disaster. I need your design expertise."

"Oh, right. The decorating project." With a jerk, Madison's heart regained its normal rhythm, and a hint of disappointment washed over her. *Snap out of it, Madison. This is business. And possibly a way of saving your own hide until you figure out who broke in.* She straightened in her chair. She had to stop letting his comments affect her so deeply, so quickly. Did he have any idea what he did to her heart? She hoped not.

This is why she hadn't dated much. Besides the time she spent at work, she knew her heart was too fragile. She soaked in his compliments like a dry sponge—it was better to keep her heart distant. Men disappointed—her father had shown how inevitable that truth was.

"Naturally, a *schones engel* like you will only further contribute to the scenery." Carsten winked as he slipped the credit card into the bill.

A blush crept over Madison's cheeks and she ducked her head, hoping to keep the compliment a safe distance from her heart. She remembered enough of her high school German lessons to know what he thought she was beautiful.

As she followed Carsten out of the restaurant and into a cab, she once again wondered if she was doing the right thing. She didn't have many other options. She didn't want to bring her dad into this if she didn't have to, and staying with Shan wouldn't garner much more security than staying alone. She had to trust her instincts—and Carsten.

Then again, her instincts had been wrong before.

6

Madison unlocked her apartment door with unsteady fingers and motioned for Carsten to go in first. Never again would she take for granted stepping into her home with a feeling of safety. Her naïvety was gone for good.

"Those must have been some tidy ransackers," Carsten joked as he stepped inside and looked around the spotlessly clean apartment.

Madison shook her head at his attempt at humor and made haste gathering her belongings. "I put everything back together after the police left. I wanted to try to find out what the intruder was looking for and had to clean up to see if anything was missing." She dragged a suitcase from the hall closet, then disappeared around the corner to her bedroom.

Carsten remained in the living area while they blindly continued their conversation. "And what did you find?"

"Nothing!" Madison slammed a drawer shut. The protesting screech of the metal slide as she flung open a second drawer punctuated her frustration. She emptied the contents into her bag. "Which must have been exactly what they found as well, because nothing was stolen."

Madison hurried back into the living room,

tucking her messy hair behind her ears as she pulled the suitcase behind her. Carsten reached for the handle while Madison grabbed a duffel bag and filled it with various colored folders.

"Work stuff," she explained at his glance. "I keep my different design layouts in these." She held up a file folder before cramming it into her duffel.

"Seems like a professional system you have there," Carsten teased.

Madison zipped the bag with an air of authority. "My system works, so call it what you will." She hoisted the bag in her arms.

"Allow me." Carsten shouldered the heavy bag.

"I think that's it."

"Ready, then?"

Madison let her eyes roam around her apartment one more time, which didn't really feel like home at the moment, and then nodded slowly.

"I suppose I am."

~*~

Madison jerked awake. She blinked against her blurry vision and rubbed damp palms down the legs of her pants. She tried to take a deep breath, but felt as if a weight sat on her shoulders, crushing her under its burden. Had she had a nightmare? Anxiety pressed hard.

"You're OK," a familiar voice soothed. A warm hand brushed the hair off her forehead. "Deep breaths."

Starting under the touch, Madison blinked again and took in the scene around her. From the cramped seating and the view out the window, she realized she was on an airplane, thousands of miles in the air. She tried to fight back the panic attack that tempted to take over. She hated flying.

Where was she going?

Bending over at the waist as far as her uncomfortable airline seat would allow, Madison continued taking deep breaths. *What time is it? What day is it?*

A full minute passed before she realized the flight attendant and her cart had rolled by and someone was pressing a cool cloth to the back of her neck.

Madison suddenly sat upright as the events of the previous twenty-four hours rushed into her memory. She twisted in her seat and saw that he was the one holding the moist towel.

"Are you all right now?"

Madison closed her eyes, torn between sinking into the comfort he offered and running from it as fast as she could. Never in her life had someone been so concerned about her well-being. Her parents' affections had always had an ulterior motive. *You can't get sick before the big party, Madison... Everyone who is anyone will be there... We can't have you being the only debutante stuck at home...You'll never make the Society Page that way, dear...*

Madison opened her eyes to rid the memories and focused on Carsten, who gazed at her as if she were the only woman in the world. *Easy, Madison. You still don't really know this man.*

A that fact seemed irrelevant when he stared at her with that clear blue gaze.

"Are you all right now?" Carsten repeated.

Madison nodded slowly and found that the longer she looked at Carsten, the less the headache pounded in her temples. She took the cloth he offered and pressed the cool rag to her forehead.

"Yes, I'm still just a little confused." She looked out the window. "What time is it?" The view proved it was late.

"It's well after midnight. You slept hard." Carsten lifted a hand as if to touch her face, and then quickly dropped it to his side. "I'm glad you're feeling better. Soon, we'll be *heim*. Home."

Madison settled back in her seat and continued to gaze out the window. With so many clouds and only a sliver of moon lighting the sky, her view of the earth below was limited. She wondered what "heim" looked like. At this point in her life, she didn't know of any place on earth she would truly call home. And why did she feel so comfortable with Carsten but like a stranger at her father's plantation in Georgia?

Shaking off the reflective thoughts, Madison tried to enjoy the rest of her flight and relax. She needed rest; her tense muscles were evidence enough of that. Worrying would have to wait.

Three hours later, Madison and Carsten were buckled in a rental car and zipping down the winding country roads toward the ranch.

Madison took in the view with awe. She had traveled all over the world, but nothing compared to the beauty of the massive expanse of sky that surrounded her on all sides. Hills and flatlands stretched as far as the eye could see. She rolled down the Jeep's window and let the wind toss her hair. Sucking in a breath of the crisp early morning air, she caught a taste of true freedom. Delicious. She wanted more.

Madison leaned her head back and closed her eyes, her elbow resting on the open window, fingers weaving in and out of the wind. She wove a random pattern with the breeze, content to relax and let the moment sink in. She was safe here. Nothing could touch her.

7

"We're here," Carsten said several minutes later. Before Madison had even unbuckled her seatbelt he was outside, opening the door and ushering her out of the vehicle. He grabbed the luggage and led the way up the massive porch to the front door.

Madison spun in a slow circle on the porch, eyes wide. Everything seemed larger than life, from the driveway that stretched half a mile to the porch swing that looked as if it could comfortably hold four adults. She felt tiny in comparison.

"This way." Carsten held the screen door open for her with his foot, his arms full of their bags. Madison hurried inside, only to stop and gaze around in wonder once again.

"Nice place, huh?" Carsten grinned at her as he set the luggage in the entryway and flicked a switch on the wall. Soft, warm lighting instantly filled the room. Madison's heart lit up along with it, and she reveled in the sense of home. *Home? That's crazy. I've been here thirty seconds.* Still, something tugged at her spirit.

"Welcome to the Running R ranch." Carsten glanced around and then shot Madison the grin that had gotten her there in the first place. "You can see why I need you to fix it up."

Madison shifted into professional mode, and cast a trained eye around the premises. The entryway led into an open, airy living space, with the kitchen to the left, the dining room and hallway leading to more rooms on the right. An indoor balcony was built over the living area, with beautiful staircases descending each side. Everything about the room, including most of the furniture, was bare wood, but it offered a homey, rustic feel. There was definite potential.

Madison's pulse quickened as ideas flowed through her mind. A touch of greenery in that corner, a splash of color on that wall...She grinned.

"I think I've created a monster." Carsten laughed. "Why don't we get settled for the night? I know you will have a dozen ideas in that pretty head of yours after a good rest."

After grabbing Madison's suitcases, Carsten started toward the living space. "Rita? Are you here? We are *heim*, Rita!"

"Carsten, is that you?" A short and sturdy woman hurried out of the kitchen, dusting her hands on the back pockets of her jeans. She looked to be in her mid-sixties, but it was hard to tell for sure, because she was covered in flour.

A smile lit her face as she recognized Carsten. "Child, it's been years! You look just like your father." She grabbed Carsten in a hug and exclaimed over him like a long lost relative.

"You're looking great, Rita." Carsten returned her hug warmly. "It's good to be back. It's been too long."

"And you must be Madison." Rita took Madison's hand in hers and pumped her arm with more energy than Madison thought possible from such a small woman. "I've been expecting you!"

"You have?" Madison shot a questioning look at Carsten.

"Rita runs this place," Carsten explained, looping an arm around the older woman's shoulders. "She's been like a grandmother to me. I would spend many summers here during my childhood visiting with my father and Mr. Sanders."

"I've kept this place together for almost twenty years now." Rita lifted her chin proudly.

Madison smiled. Rita's charm and energy was contagious. She made everything seem joyful just by being in her presence.

"How are you handling the loss?" Carsten's voice dropped to a softer level as he kept his arm around Rita and turned her toward the kitchen.

Madison followed at a distance but couldn't help overhearing their conversation.

"It's been hard, certainly, but the joy of the Lord is my strength." Rita blinked several times as she turned on the oven light to check its contents. "I know I was just the hired help, but Andrew was like family to me." She lowered her voice. "I still miss your father, too, of course. How are you—"

Carsten cleared his throat, interrupting. "Rita, you know better than that. Andrew loved you. You were never just the hired help."

Rita smiled sadly as she grabbed a flowered mitt and went to pull the fresh bread from the oven. "I guess I do know that."

Carsten turned his head near Madison's ear to explain. "Andrew Sanders is the man who passed on recently and left the estate to my family. The legal procedures were completed last week and this has been the first chance I have had to see the ranch since."

Madison stood silently as the details sunk in. Then she turned, confused, to question Carsten. "But why should I redecorate everything if Rita lives here? Shouldn't she have a decision in that?"

Carsten smirked and leaned back against the counter.

"Land sakes!" Rita let the oven door slam shut with a bang. She turned, her mitted hands holding a tray of hot bread, and stared at Madison. "How do you suppose I have time to decorate this monstrosity of a house in between all of my baking and cooking and shopping and cleaning? You must be a stranger to ranch life, indeed." Her wink softened her harsh words as she dropped the tray on the stovetop.

"Now, you hear me!" Rita's tirade continued, loud and exaggerated and somehow still entirely friendly. "Mr. Sanders was a sweet man but knew absolutely squat about how a home should look. He wanted everything just as bare and simple as it could be. After Judy left him all those years ago, he just let the house go. Didn't seem to care what it looked like anymore. After that, he spent all his time outside with those animals of his. Guess he figured horses were safer than people."

Rita picked up each biscuit and dropped the steaming bread into a cloth-covered basket. "Now, I know Mr. Sanders is no longer able to enjoy my good home cookin', God bless his soul, but I still have a bunch of cowboys to feed. Those horses and cattle still have to be tended to. Someone has to make sure things run smoothly around here. I know that Mitch Hawkins is the foreman and thinks he's the boss of everything in creation, but I know better.

If I didn't feed those poor men working out there, why, they'd be thinner than a cat's tail and just as ugly." Rita paused for a breath.

Madison wasn't sure if she was supposed to respond, so she glanced at Carsten.

"Rita, I think Ms. Lawrence is in need of some sleep. We've had a long flight. Why don't you show her to her room and we'll catch up further over lunch."

"Of course! I'm so sorry, darlin', I didn't even think about you having that nasty jetlag. I haven't flown in years and don't intend to. This ranch is my home, I have no reason to leave." Rita rambled on as she grabbed one of Madison's bags and kept right on going toward the living room staircase.

Although Madison felt certain her ears would start bleeding any given moment with Rita's constant chatter, she enjoyed the woman's warmth and attention. Madison had never met anyone like the older dynamo. She felt an instant kinship with this kind woman and hoped they'd be able to get better acquainted during her brief stay at the ranch.

"This will be your room right here." Rita turned left at the top of the balcony and opened the first door to the right. "You'll have a nice view."

Madison stepped inside the room and tried not to grimace. The view was indeed spectacular, but it was the only focal point of the space. The walls were white, the floor bare wood, the bed draped in white sheets with a white quilt folded at the end. No pictures adorned the walls, no curtains decorated the window, no rugs on the floor. The small dresser and nightstand, along with the frame of the bed, were all made of plain wood, not even polished or stained. The entire room looked as if it had been carved out of a giant log and pieced together.

"It's nice." Madison turned a grateful smile to Rita and reached to bring her suitcases inside. Instead, she bumped into Carsten, who was already rolling them in.

"I hope you'll be comfortable here. I can't wait to see what you do with this place. It needs a womanly touch, and I'm definitely not the woman for that job!" Rita smiled then breezed out of the room.

Standing in the bedroom beside Carsten, Madison ignored the funny quiver in her stomach. She took a step closer to the window, and the view immediately distracted her—however briefly—from his presence.

"Wow," she breathed. The morning sun lit up the pastures below like golden dew. Rolling hills and plains stretched on for miles, until finally hitting the base of the mountains. She didn't see a single fence marking property lines, and she wondered exactly how many acres Carsten now owned.

"They're working the horses out that way." Carsten joined her at the window and pointed toward the barn. Several men wearing cowboy hats were on horseback inside the corral swinging lassos.

Madison's eyes drank in the sight. She had been in the city far too long. The sight of green grass and animals was already doing wonders for her spirit. She closed her eyes briefly. *Thanks, Lord. I guess you knew what you were doing after all.*

"I bet they'd let you ride if you asked nicely."

Madison opened her eyes and balked. "I like to watch from a distance. Animals taller than my knee make me nervous up close."

Carsten grinned and shook his head. "I'll make a country girl out of you yet."

Madison smiled back at him and lifted her chin. "I wouldn't bet on it."

"We'll have to wait and see." He chucked her lightly on the chin with his fist.

Madison's face warmed at his touch and she kept her eyes trained on the pastures below. She knew that if she turned to meet his gaze, she would want to kiss him. *He might not even want your kiss.* That was so long ago...But the memory of that enchanted night held her captive.

"I'll leave so you can rest. Rita will have lunch ready around noon. If you're awake in time, come eat with us." Carsten turned to go and Madison followed him with her gaze.

"I won't turn down a good home cooked meal." Madison grinned and tried to ignore the feelings that rose in her heart.

Carsten paused in the doorway and studied her for a minute. "Then sleep well, *mein engel.*"

8

Carsten sat perched on a barstool, resting his elbows on the counter in Rita's kitchen just as he had all those summers ago. This time, his feet touched the floor.

"I know what you need." Rita shot him a knowing look and inched the cookie jar closer. Carsten grinned and helped himself, pulling out a handful of sugar cookies.

"Some things never change." Rita poured him a glass of milk.

"I should be too old for cookies and milk." He punctuated his response by shoving half a cookie into his mouth. "But it's one of those days," he mumbled around the treat.

"You never were a drinking man, were you?" Rita's question was more like a statement. "I guess some vices are worse than others. This one might make you chubby, but at least you'll keep your head on your shoulders." She poked a finger against his flat stomach and laughed.

Carsten shook his head. "Rita, how did I make it through so many years without seeing you?" The woman had been his rock during the time after his father passed away. She'd sent letters and care packages for weeks after the funeral, even called to check on him in the months following. No one else had made the same effort.

Rita waved off his comment with a flick of her hand. She grabbed a dishtowel and began swiping at a pretend mark on the already spotless counter.

"It's been at least ten years." Carsten took a swig of milk. He stared into space as he mentally turned back pages on the calendar of his life. His last visit to the Running R had been when he was about to turn seventeen. He remembered that visit well. It was the last time he had ever gone fishing with his father. He missed those carefree summers. He always felt privileged that his dad had chosen to bring him on visits to the United States to see Andrew. His mother had never wanted to come, and Carsten realized now in hindsight that his mom knew how important that father-son time was to each of them. He felt a surge of gratitude, followed by a twinge of remorse. But this was not the time to think about the past.

"Rita, I don't know if I told you the whole story about Madison." Carsten spoke softly. He darted a glance over his shoulder to make sure the kitchen door was shut and turned his gaze to the woman he trusted more than any other.

Rita stopped her cleaning and took the stool next to him. "You told me yesterday that you were going to bring Ms. Lawrence here for her own safety. Some men are after her, and her father wanted her out of harm's way until the matter could be resolved."

"That's right." Carsten ran a hand through his hair and sighed deeply. "But Madison doesn't know that. As I told you before, she thinks she's here simply on a decorating project. She's aware there is something going on, but has no idea of what. Her apartment was ransacked and she was followed yesterday, but she has yet to fully grasp the severity of the situation."

Rita nodded slowly. "I see."

"It gets worse." Carsten let out a breath. "She doesn't know her father hired me to protect her. She thinks I just showed up at the right place in the right time. In fact, she called me. I think she believes this entire incident is one big coincidence."

"But you really do want the ranch decorated," Rita argued.

"That was my original intent, yes And while there is definitely work for her to do while she is here, it's also now part of the ruse. Her father heard of the ransacking from the police immediately after it happened. He has deep connections and equally deep pockets. He called me at Angel Enterprises, said he knew Dad from years ago. He named an obscene amount of money that would be mine if I convinced Madison to travel to Montana with me and keep her safe for a few weeks. He suggested she stay until things settle down in New York. The only catch is that Mr. Lawrence doesn't want Madison to know he hired me. He knows how Madison would react."

"It sounds as if she's the independent type. I'm surprised you got her here at all." Rita drummed her nails on the counter top. "But why would he lie to his own daughter?"

"I'm not sure." Carsten frowned. "But I do know that there will be trouble if she finds out. He hinted at that much. I have a feeling that Madison's relationship with her father isn't ideal."

Rita narrowed her eyes. "So who is after her,

and why?"

"That's another question I can't answer."

"There seem to be several of those."

"I wish there weren't. I do know that I'd die before I'd let anything happen to Madison."

Rita's eyebrows shot up. Carsten realized too late that he had said too much.

"That sure is a passionate statement considering how you've only known the woman for a few days."

Carsten ducked his head and knew he better confess all. "There's more to the story." He traced a pattern in the Formica with his thumbnail.

Rita waited silently.

"I've met Madison before, several years ago in Germany."

Rita's mouth dropped in surprise.

"I was out for a walk one night when this...this angel appeared before me in the courtyard. She was a vision. It was long ago; she must have been about eighteen at the time. I just know that when I saw her, I couldn't breathe."

Even now, six years later, his heartbeat doubled in rhythm at the memory. "I had to see her again. Even as all the years passed by, her face haunted my dreams. I ran a search and discovered she was an interior designer with a business based in New York. So, I took the easy way out and let her believe that I desperately needed her decorating services."

"So you're telling me that you met this woman in Germany and now all these years later you're being hired to protect her? Does her father know you've met her before?" Rita's eyes were opened wide.

Carsten shook his head. "That part was strictly a

coincidence. He contacted my firm, asking for a favor. I agreed to take the job. Mr. Lawrence thinks the reason that I was already in the U.S. when he called me was strictly because of my wanting to visit the ranch after the inheritance. He has no idea that I was in New York and had already contacted Madison when he called."

"Hmm. Now that is something. Seems to me like God's hand was in that crazy set-up." Rita sat up straighter on her stool and shook her head. "You're in for quite a ride, my boy. I thought you'd have enough trouble dealing with a city girl here on this ranch for a month or so. I never once imagined that you'd already be in love with her."

"*Liebe*?" Carsten coughed. He shook his head quickly. "I barely know her. I can't be in love. She's just…different than other women." To put it mildly. Madison, while beautiful outwardly, carried something inside her that he'd immediately noticed that fateful night.

And had yet to forget.

Rita pursed her lips. "Mmhhmm."

"No, Rita." Carsten eased off the stool and began wiping up his cookie crumbs. "I don't need you putting any ideas in my head." He dusted his hands off over the sink.

"It's not what I'm putting in your head, dear boy. It's what God has already put in your heart."

Rita's words lingered in Carsten's mind throughout the rest of the morning, as he lay tossing and turning on the bed in the downstairs guestroom. Was she right? Did he love Madison already? He barely knew her, yet he could not deny the strong attraction that pulsed through his veins every time he saw the woman, or thought about her. Had God put them together? That was ridiculous. God had better things to do than worry about Carsten Erlichman's love life.

And Carsten had better things to do than worry about love. Like keep Madison alive—which would be a lot easier to do if he knew who was after her, and why.

Turning over on his side, Carsten punched his pillow and tried to get comfortable. Yet the word love kept playing over and over in his thoughts.

Tired of fighting it, Carsten rolled onto his back, crossed his arms under his head, and stared at the ceiling. He knew that somewhere up on the second floor, the most beautiful woman he had ever met slept peacefully, completely naïve to both her perilous situation and his feelings.

He wondered grimly which of the two was the most dangerous.

9

Madison woke to the sound of a cowbell. Thinking she imagined it, she rolled over and tried to drift back to sleep. The few hours of rest she'd had, had definitely not been enough to catch her up from the midnight flight.

Clang clang CLANG!

Madison jerked and realized with a start that the cowbell was real. Feeling like an Army recruit, Madison leapt out of bed and frantically tried to remember where she was and why there was such a commotion.

The view out her window reminded her of her whereabouts and calmed her nerves. She turned to fix her hair and realized that there wasn't one mirror in the entire room. Maybe she should focus on decorating her temporary bedroom before she got to work on the rest of the house.

Clang CLANG!

Madison winced. She thought lunch had been optional. Apparently, Rita was ready for her and Carsten to join her. Her stomach rumbled, and she realized she was hungry after all.

Deciding to forget about her rumpled appearance, Madison hurried downstairs before Rita could ring the bell again.

She entered the kitchen just in time to see Carsten, hair mussed from sleep, trying to wrestle the torturous instrument from Rita.

Laughing, the older woman surrendered the bell. "I had to call in the men from the stables. Plus, you city folks need a taste of country-life." Rita straightened her blouse and ignored Carsten's triumphant look as he placed the bell on top of the refrigerator where she wouldn't be able to reach it again.

"Lunch is on." Rita nodded toward the door and ushered them into the dining room.

"Rita, you made all of my favorites! You remembered." Carsten shot an appreciative glance over the table laden with food.

Madison's gaze roved over the numerous items, mentally comparing the calorie contents of her typical lunchtime salad with the gigantic bowls full of peas, beans, mashed potatoes, corn on the cob, and juicy fried chicken strips.

"And don't forget the biscuits." Rita placed a steaming basket of homemade bread on the center of the table next to the gallon-sized tub of butter.

Madison gulped. She would surely turn into a pig before she returned to New York City. She was trying to figure out how to bow out of the heavy meal graciously when Carsten pulled out a chair and ushered her into it.

"This looks great, Rita," Madison said, pasting a smile to her lips. How would she eat a tub of butter without having it stick to her thighs? No way came to mind, so she mentally shrugged and decided that if she was going to gain weight, she might as well enjoy herself along the way. She began to load her plate.

Suddenly, the dining room filled with a herd of

a dozen cowboys. Madison stared in shock as the men jockeyed for position around the table and began removing their hats. One particularly tall man noticed Madison with surprise, and nudged the guy beside him, who also turned to stare. "Well hello, there lil' darlin'.

Several of the men then sent curious glances in her direction.

Madison nodded at him in response, and then ducked her head to study the beans on her plate. *I guess that nap didn't mess up my hair very badly after all.*

"And who might you be?" The tall man spoke again, pulling out the chair opposite Madison and studying her with a dark, overly interested gaze.

"That's enough, Mitch." Rita scolded from the other end of the table. Madison remembered Rita mentioning Mitch's name earlier. *He thinks he's the boss over all creation.* Madison made a mental note to steer clear of him.

Before things went any further, Carsten cleared his throat. "This is Madison. She is an interior designer hired temporarily at the Running R. I trust you will treat her as honorably as any other guest." He waited for the murmurs of assent to ripple through the cowboys.. "Now, let's give thanks." Carsten bowed his head, and the other men followed suit—except for Mitch who boldly continued to hold Madison's gaze.

Madison stared, still in shock. She was used to receiving appreciative glances on the streets in New York, but Mitch turned her stomach. She bit her lip and told herself that she was safe. If Carsten didn't think these men were dangerous, then they weren't.

She was just jumpy because of the break-in.

The prayer ended and Madison realized with a shock that she hadn't caught a word of it. She offered a silent blessing over her food and began to eat.

Madison ate silently, trying to blend in. The last thing she wanted right now was attention. Between bites, Madison caught snippets of Carsten's conversation with the men closest to him. The workers knew that Carsten now owned the ranch, and it sounded as if several of them were concerned about their jobs. Madison smiled as she listened to the gentle assurance Carsten doled out. No one would be fired if he had his way.

"Ahem!"

Too late, Madison realized that Rita had been trying to get her attention for quite some time while she'd been watching Carsten. Fighting back a telltale blush, she turned her gaze to the older woman. "I'm sorry, I was just day dreaming."

Rita's lips pursed. "Mmhmmm. I was going to suggest that Carsten take you out on the ranch after lunch. I know he'd like to refresh his memory of the land. Maybe a horseback riding tour would be just the thing."

Madison felt something jump in her stomach at the thought of getting on a horse. Clearing her throat, Madison pasted on a smile. "I haven't...ever really, you know...ridden... before."

Rita grinned behind her glass of tea. "There's a first time for everything."

Nope. Not today there wasn't.

Madison nodded politely and picked up her own glass.

"Do I hear some plotting going on?" Carsten broke into their conversation. "I'd love to go riding with you, Madison."

She opened her mouth to protest, but Carsten continued.

"You might get some inspiration for your designs. The countryside is beautiful."

Madison knew he had her cornered. She figured he knew it as well.

"Sounds great," she lied. *Great. Now what?*

Madison watched as Rita sat back in her chair, looking overly pleased with the results of the conversation. Interesting. What was she up to? She made a vow to observe the woman carefully for the remainder of her stay. Because the last thing her heart needed was someone playing the role of matchmaker.

~*~

An hour later, Madison found herself inside the stables. She tried to ignore the nervous twinge attempting to take over her body and followed Carsten bravely down the hay-strewn aisle to the right wing of stalls. The distinct, musty smell of hay and horses assaulted her senses, and she fought the urge to pull the collar of her shirt up over her nose.

"Pretty nice place," she commented, as much as to distract herself from what she was about to do as to compliment.

Carsten nodded, looking around proudly. "It always was. Andrew's top priority was keeping this place maintained. I used to joke with my father about how the barn was prettier than the house."

Madison cast a second look around and was

tempted to agree. The stables were very well-kept and clean. She remembered that the horses she had seen from her bedroom window were beautiful and well groomed. And large. Her professional side strove to appreciate the architecture of the barn while at the same time, her stomach churned, trying to remind her of the upcoming inevitable contact with the creatures.

Carsten gentled his tone as they stopped in front of a stall door. "This is Sasha. She's a sweet old mare. I remember riding her when I was a teenager. You won't have any problems with her."

Madison peered over the tall gate. A pretty dappled gray mare stood in the corner of the stall munching on hay. She seemed harmless enough.

Sasha ambled over to the door and stretched her neck over the top. Madison gulped and took a step back, and then realized the horse was just being curious. Madison reached out and tentatively petted Sasha's nose.

"It's so soft!" Madison grinned in spite of her apprehension.

The appreciative smile on Carsten's face gave her a burst of courage, and she ran her hand down the length of the mare's neck. This wasn't so bad.

Sasha nickered softly and went back to her hay.

"And this," Carsten began, stepping sideways to the stall neighboring Sasha's, "Is my mount, Samson."

Madison's eyes widened as she looked over the stall door and then up...up...

Samson stood in the center of his stall, neck arched proudly. He stretched taller than any horse Madison had ever seen. She had to admit he was beautiful, solid black with just enough of a white splash on his nose to give him character and remind her of her favorite children's book, *Black Beauty*.

"He's...giant." Madison whispered.

Carsten chuckled and reached out to pet the horse. Samson stood proud, as if acknowledging Carsten's presence would be too far below him. After a moment of coaxing, the horse walked just close enough to the stall door to allow brief contact with Carsten's outstretched hand.

"He was born here on the ranch during one of my visits. Andrew let me take care of him while I was here." Memory clouded Carsten's eyes, and Madison bit her lower lip. She knew how he felt.

"He's got fire. I have several people interested in buying him already. They think he'd make an excellent stud horse." Carsten studied the stallion before turning back to meet Madison's gaze. "And he would. But I could never part with him."

Madison softened at the love she saw between the man and his horse. That was something she didn't get to see in the city. She smiled. Maybe this wouldn't be so bad after all.

Carsten slapped his hand against the top of the stall door and faced Madison. "Before you leave the ranch, you'll be riding him like a real cowboy, lil' missy," he said with an exaggerated cowboy drawl that sounded completely ridiculous combined with his natural German accent.

Madison shook her head, and her hair swished in front of her face. "No way." She'd be doing good just to get on Sasha.

Carsten reached out to brush the flyaway strands of her hair back into place. The moment his fingers touched her cheek, their gazes locked and held. Madison's mouth opened, but she forgot how to breathe. She imagined herself back in Germany, once more in a beautiful courtyard, dancing on a fountain wall with the man of her dreams.

Carsten's eyes darkened to a shade of blue she had only seen in a winter sky. His hand slid back to cup her neck in his palm. He began to pull her closer, and Madison's stomach dipped again, this time for a completely different reason.

The touch of his lips on hers sent a rivulet of contentment down her spine. She felt so at home in his arms.

Suddenly, Samson let loose an indignant whinny, and Carsten released her abruptly. Madison's heart sank. She blinked, wondering how Carsten could have possibly backed away that fast. Her lips still tingled from his nearness, and her heart shouted in confusion. What just happened?

Carsten turned toward Samson's stall, bracing his arms against the top of the door. He ran a hand through his hair and took a ragged breath. "I'm sorry." He hung his head and then after a moment, turned to face her. Looking straight into Madison's eyes, he apologized again. "I shouldn't have done that."

Madison nodded jerkily, turning to face Samson. It was easier than looking into Carsten's face and wondering why he thought he had to ask forgiveness for a simple kiss. She frowned in confusion. It wasn't as if it were their first. Did he not remember that magical moment in Germany? They'd never discussed it. Maybe he didn't. Maybe that night had meant nothing to him.

Sorrow shot tiny arrows into Madison's heart. She glanced at Carsten. He seemed to be waiting for a response. She cleared her throat and shook back her hair. "No problem." She forced a quick smile then turned her attention back to the horse in front of her. Maybe he was right—kisses would only make things more confusing right now. She was here to work, not for romance.

She fed Samson a handful of hay, all the while her heart crying out. *Change the subject already! Say something, anything…*

Carsten dusted his hands off on his back pockets. "How about we get them saddled and ride on out?"

Madison, despite her fear, found herself ready to agree. Riding, as scary as it might be, had to be better than their current awkward situation. She straightened her shoulders and nodded.

~*~

Carsten mentally kicked himself as he lifted the supple leather saddle onto Samson's back. He cast a glance over his shoulder at Madison, who stood outside the stall door, staring off into space. She looked confused—or scared. Had he put that look in her eye, or was it already there? She had been nervous about riding—but something told him this was more than that.

Biting back a groan, he tightened the girth strap on the saddle, pressing his knee into Samson's side so he'd release the stubborn breath of air that kept his saddle loose. Carsten had learned that lesson once the hard way. Luckily, only his pride had been bruised.

He lifted each of Samson's hooves, checking for lodged stones or rocks that would make him uncomfortable during their ride. As he lifted Samson's back leg, the stallion leaned heavily against him, pushing his weight into Carsten's shoulder. Carsten pushed back. Didn't he have enough of a burden already? He quickly secured the bridle, then opened the stall gate and led Samson out into the aisle.

Madison quickly shuffled backward, eyes wide. Had she moved away from him or from the horse?

"Don't worry, Samson is perfectly safe to be near," he said, hoping it was the horse she was afraid of. "Just no sudden movements by his head. And don't walk directly behind him."

Carsten smiled, but Madison's expression didn't change. What had he done? He didn't want her to fear him, but he supposed he couldn't really blame her. He was forever stealing kisses. No wonder she was so stiff. When would he learn?

Their chemistry, though, was so tangible that it practically pulsed right between them in the barn — And at the house. And on the plane. And wherever they were together — unable to be denied.

But he had to start denying it, or Maddie wouldn't last three days out here with him, much less long enough for him to figure out how to keep her safe.

He looped the reins around the post outside the barn door, and went back to prepare Sasha for the ride. Madison stayed near the stall door.

He definitely shouldn't have crossed that line again. He was a professional, nothing more than the hired help from her father. That meant she was off limits, no matter what her eyes did to his heart. He'd do good to remember that.

He had no doubt Teddy Lawrence would enjoy reminding him.

~*~

Several minutes later, Madison found herself balanced precariously on Sasha's back, one hand gripping the reins, the other wrapped so tightly around the saddle horn that she had already lost feeling in her fingers.

"Relax." Carsten was suddenly standing beside Sasha. Madison glanced down. Her knee was even with Carsten's chest. She knew Sasha wasn't that big of a horse, especially compared to Samson, but at the moment, she was felt as if she sitting in the sky.

"How is that possible when I'm on this...this...gigantic beast?" Madison hesitated, and then corrected herself. "Sweet beast, I meant." She didn't want Sasha to become offended and decide to throw her off.

Carsten ducked his head, but Madison caught the grin he tried to hide. She appreciated the effort to cover his amusement and decided to try and toughen up. If only her friends in New York could see her now. Shan would already be having a fit...

"Shan!" Madison's eyes opened wide as she realized that she had yet to inform her friend and partner of her whereabouts. Shan would be worried sick that she hadn't come in to work

Carsten's jaw dropped. "You haven't called her yet?

Madison slumped down in the saddle. "I never thought about it after I woke up from my nap. She probably thinks I'm sick. I bet I have a hundred missed calls on my cellphone."

"If she's waited this long, she can wait another hour. Let's go while the horses are ready. I'll remind you to call her once we get back to the house." Carsten took charge of the situation and Madison surprisingly found herself letting him. She decided to ponder that thought later, and turned her full attention back to the horse underneath her.

10

Carsten pointed Samson toward the south, and Madison followed on Sasha, barely daring to breathe. Sasha snorted and tossed her head, as if sensing Madison's nervousness. She danced a side step, and Madison shrieked.

"You have to relax, Maddie." Madison started at the nickname and looked up to see Carsten twisted around in his saddle, eyeing her over his shoulder.

"Sasha can tell how you feel. If you relax, she'll relax. You're making her nervous."

"I'm making her nervous?" Madison repeated incredulously. Nevertheless, she took a deep, shaky breath and relaxed her muscles. Sasha snorted again and then calmly walked forward after Samson.

Madison kept a tight grip on the saddle horn, but found herself relaxing more and more with each step. The farther they moved from the ranch house, the more beautiful and wild the scenery became. Wildflowers took over the meadow that stretched for miles, dotting the acreage with shades of purple, yellow and pink. Rolling hills led to the mountains in the distance, standing firm against the sea of green. Springtime was kind to Montana.

She raised her hand to shield her eyes from the sun as the horses turned uphill. She noticed that Carsten rode easily, as if he had been born in the saddle. He made it look so simple.

Reaching forward, Madison dared to pat Sasha's neck. The mare tossed her head and nickered softly. Madison caught herself smiling.

So why couldn't the people in her life respond to her affection the same?

~*~

Carsten turned in his saddle to check on Madison, and smiled at the scene behind him. He felt a surge of pride over the way she had risen to the challenge. She looked much more comfortable in the saddle compared to an hour earlier. A gust of wind blew over the hills, and lifted Madison's blonde hair. The sight instantly took him back to a cold night in Germany, where the sudden appearance of a blonde angel had taken his breath away.

Carsten loosened the reins and let Samson have his head as he revisited his favorite memory of all time. That night had been magical. There had been something in the air, whether it was a whisper of the future or a gift from God, Carsten wasn't certain, but it had been there, just as tangible as the ground beneath his feet as he had walked home from the office that snowy night.

He had been in a foul mood. His work weighed heavily on his mind. Ever since his father's passing, all burdens had fallen to his shoulders. It was a tiresome load, and it was all he'd been able to think about as he'd headed for his apartment. He wasn't sure what had coaxed him to take a new route home that evening, but he had followed the urging inside. It had led him to the clock tower in the courtyard. Even as an adult, he liked to gaze at the tower. It took him back to his childhood, and reminded him of the stories his mother used to read at bedtime, back before he grew up, before life became so complicated.

It was only fitting that he would experience his own fairy tale there in the same courtyard. Madison had appeared with the wind that evening, shivering inside her coat, a vision in a red dress that celebrated the coming holiday. Carsten remembered the evening like it was yesterday, not six long years ago.

He smiled to himself. Madison had found him to be smooth and charming. She couldn't have known that his insides were shaking, and it was all he could do to even speak. But something had calmed his heart as he held her closely, dancing on that fountain wall. Never before had he been that impulsive. His type of business drove him to be cautious, alert, punctual and rational, not…romantic. People got hurt if he got distracted.

Carsten glanced over his shoulder again Madison had her face lifted to the wind, and the sun made her hair shine golden.

He couldn't deny that the attraction was still there. Time had done nothing but increase his feelings for her. Carsten hoped she felt the same. But how could he pursue a relationship under the current circumstances? He was to keep her safe, not break her heart.

Carsten jerked back to reality as Samson began to jog beneath him. He had given the stallion his head for too long, and now the horse was eager to run. He pulled back on the reins to slow Samson's gait. He didn't want Sasha to follow suit and start running with Madison unprepared…

A grey and blonde flash flew past him, a high-pitched shriek drifting in its wake. Too late, Carsten realized that Sasha's competitive streak wasn't going to let a horse run in front of her and get away with it. He knew from experience that Sasha now considered herself officially in a race. This was not what he had in mind when he promised Madison that she would have no problems with her mount. He quickly nudged Samson with his knees and started after the runaway duo.

"Help!" Madison's shrill cry of distress was distinct over the pounding of hooves.

Carsten urged Samson to run faster. He bent low over the saddle, yelling over the rushing wind. "Hang on Madison!"

"Do you think I'm going to let go?" Her sarcastic response made him smile in spite of the dangerous circumstances. At least she still had her sense of humor. He reached out as Samson came alongside the runaway mare and grabbed Sasha's bridle.

"Whoa there, girl." He pulled back on Samson's reins, knowing that as soon as the stallion slowed, Sasha would follow suit. The mare snorted her distaste for being asked to stop running, but reluctantly came to a walk.

"Maybe you should get down for a minute," Carsten suggested, noticing Madison's trembling posture. Her eyes narrowed as her grip on the saddle horn tightened even further.

Carsten helped her down from the saddle. Once her feet were planted firmly in the grass, he took one of her hands in his. "You're way too tense." He began to massage her palms.

She slumped against his weight, eyes half shut.

Carsten directed her to the shade, where he settled her against the trunk of the tree. "I hope you still want to ride back."

Madison leaned her head back against the bark and shut her eyes. "That's a bridge I might not cross." She rubbed a shaky hand over her face, smudging dirt across her nose.

Carsten reached out automatically and brushed the smear away, his hand lingering on her cheek.

Madison cleared her throat and abruptly averted her gaze. Carsten felt the pain of her rejection and dropped his hand. He deserved it, after the stolen kiss in the stables, but it still stung.

"Carsten…"

"Maddie…"

They laughed, interrupting the awkward moment.

"Ladies first." Carsten plucked a blade of grass from the ground and rolled it between his fingers.

Madison took a deep breath. "No, you."

Carsten studied her with an inquisitive stare until she finally looked away.

"We need to have a discussion about your current situation. There are questions that need answering, ideas that need to be formed, and arrangements that should be made. We need plans and back up options." Carsten hesitated as he realized how official he sounded.

Madison tilted her head. "How do you know so much about this?"

Carsten fought not to give anything away in his expression. "Common sense." He figured his degree in criminal justice and a lifetime of learning from his father, a private investigator, didn't need to be mentioned. The truth could wait. Perhaps indefinitely.

"Do you think I'm in real danger?" Madison's eyes widened, and she wiped her palms down her jeans.

Carsten fumbled for the right words. He wanted to be honest with Madison, but not frighten her. The fear in her eyes tugged at his heart. He wished he had never promised Teddy he would keep his services a secret. He took a deep breath. "To be honest, I have no idea what we're dealing with. Right now, the only facts we have are that someone ransacked your apartment and tried to follow your cab to work."

"Right." Madison nodded. "And then it seemed like someone shot out the tires of the SUV that was chasing me."

Carsten gulped. "That's assumption," he corrected. No sense in Madison knowing that it was his gun that had stopped the SUV from following her. She had no need to know that he had already been on duty protecting her before she had even called him that night. "It's possible a tire blew on its own accord."

Madison shrugged. "Either way, I feel that God sent my guardian angel to protect me." She shivered.

Carsten smiled and hoped he showed no signs of his inner struggle. He believed in God, that much was certain. But in his line of work, it was a little harder to blindly trust. He had seen too much, too many times. Guardian angels didn't always show up in time, and Carsten found it difficult to understand how God could allow such horrible things to happen to good people. It was a battle he struggled with daily, but he had no desire to begin fighting it now.

He pushed the thoughts of doubt out of his mind and focused on Madison. God had put Madison back in his life. At least part of him believed that. The other part wondered. Was she a gift?

More like a cruel joke. She was off-limits.

"I'm safe at the ranch, though, right?" Madison played with the ring on her right hand, twirling the silver band around and around on her finger.

Carsten knew what the nervous action meant. She wanted to believe this was no big deal, but her gut knew better. She was seeking answers from him, answers he couldn't give.

"I would never let anything happen to you." Carsten's voice thickened with emotion, and Madison looked up.

"I know." She smiled, holding his gaze.

The moment stretched until Madison stood. "So, on a lighter note," she began, brushing grass off her jeans. "When should I get started on designing? We'll need to meet together to discuss paint, wallpaper, furniture arrangements, the budget...that's why I'm here, after all."

Carsten stood as well. "Right." He echoed. "That's why you're here." His voice trailed off, and he turned back to the horses.

That would be the only reason Madison would ever know about—as long as he could help it.

~*~

After arriving back at the ranch house, Madison dug out her cellphone that was buried in her purse. Sure enough, she had twelve missed calls, all from her co-worker. Perched on the edge of her bed, she quickly dialed Shan's number and bit her lip, wondering how she should explain the situation.

Shan answered breathlessly on the second ring. "All right Ms. Thang, you have a lot of explaining to do! I know you better than to think you're on a weekend fling. What gives?"

Madison laughed. "Of course I'm not having a fling." She pushed aside the thought and got serious. "I'm in Montana, Shan. I'm with Carsten."

Shan squealed so loudly that Madison jerked the phone away from her ear. "I thought you just said you weren't having a fling!"

"I'm not," she corrected. She shook her head impatiently, as if that would help clarify the situation. "Listen, my apartment was ransacked last night. I called Carsten for help and agreed to take the design job here at his ranch. I decided it might be safer for me to leave town for a while and let things settle down." She moved the phone to her other ear. "Shan, I think I'm in some kind of danger."

"Ransacked?" Shan repeated. She paused. "What on earth would you have that someone else would want?"

Madison tried not to feel insulted even though she knew Shan was right. "That's exactly why I left. I have no idea." She sighed and flopped down on the bed into a more comfortable position. "I just knew I didn't want to stay at home."

"Why didn't you just call your father?"

Madison hesitated. "My instincts said to call

Carsten, and here I am."

"You're not usually that impulsive." Shan's voice grew suspicious. "Are you sure you don't have feelings for Mr. Hunk?"

"He's not a hunk." Madison's response was automatic, and she felt her cheeks turn red at the lie.

"Right." Shan's sarcasm was thick. "And I'm the spittin' image of Elvis Presley."

Madison giggled in spite of the tension. She missed her friend already.

"I just did what I did, for lack of a better explanation. I think God led me here, Shan."

"How long are you going to be gone?"

Madison pawed through her purse for her day planner. "I don't know; maybe for a few more weeks. I have to finish the decorating project here, regardless of what resolves back in New York. I'm trying to forget the whole incident with the break-in, to be honest. Carsten keeps insisting on bringing it back up. It's making me nervous."

"When do you plan on telling your father where you are?"

Madison bristled at the question. "I'm not a kid anymore, Shan. If my dad wants to find me, he will."

Silence once again filled the line. Madison heard her friend sigh.

"Be safe, girl. Keep me posted."

"I will." Madison promised. "I'll call you. If I'm here much longer, I might need you to mail me some things from the office. I packed in a hurry."

After saying their goodbyes, Madison hit the off button on her phone and dropped it back into her purse. She pulled a pillow into her lap and hugged it tightly. She wasn't sure if she wanted her father to find her or not. Years spent reaching for him and constantly having him push her away had taken their toll. She could only be rejected so many times. She had decided long ago that it was time to press forward. Looking back was too painful. The years she and her father spent together had been wasted. There had been too much publicity, too many parties, too much money...

And too little time.

11

Carsten watched Madison through the slit between the kitchen doors. She sat crossed legged in the chair at the oak dining table, her color-coded file folders spread around her. She absently tapped a colored pencil against her front teeth as she studied her latest sketch. He had seen enough of her sketches to know she was good. Very good. She had renovated the living room on paper, turning the balcony into a focal point and adding elaborate carvings into the banisters. According to her sketch, it really gave the room a touch of elegance while not taking away from the rustic atmosphere. He appreciated the way she tried to add without taking away.

He quietly slipped up behind her and tugged her ponytail. Madison turned with a smile as Carsten settled into the chair beside her.

"You're late."

"And you've been putting pencils in your mouth again." Carsten grinned as he reached over to wipe a smudge of green color from the corner of her lip.

They had been at the ranch for five days now, and it had been enough time to give Carsten insight into who Madison truly was, both as a person and as an artist. She was laid back, almost sloppy with her way of conducting business, but there was an organization and detail to her chaos that left him both baffled and amused. Whatever means of a system she had, it worked. Her designs were beautiful. Carsten saw many dollar signs whenever he looked at her sketches, but he knew whatever money he spent would be well worth the final effect. There was no price too high when it came to keeping Madison safe. The intensity of the feelings he had for her made him nervous. He might be able to pay any price to keep her safe, but he knew in his heart that he could never afford to lose her.

"What do you think of the banisters?" Madison rose to a sitting position on her knees in the chair, scooting the sketch closer to him.

"I think they're perfect."

"I think so, too."

"How much are they going to cost me?"

"I thought you said money was no object."

"It's not...so how much?"

Madison laughed. "I'm not sure yet. We'll need to go shopping in town soon, pick out fabrics and paint. Do you trust me to go alone?"

Carsten winced. The thought of all day shopping trip was not his idea of a productive day, but guarding Madison was his job, as well as his own personal goal, so she couldn't go alone. It wasn't an option.

"Trust a nationally recognized artist with my ranch house? You must be crazy." Carsten pushed back his chair and stood. "I'd be honored to accompany you." He swept into a bow.

Madison waved her hand to dismiss him. "Very well, carry on," she said while matching his stuffy accent. "We'll rendezvous on the morrow."

"I like the sound of that." Carsten heard his voice grow husky. He dropped to his knees on the floor beside her, moving in close. This was their first close encounter since the shared moment in the stables. He had known another was inevitable. The chemistry between them was too strong. They were like magnets fighting to stick together.

Madison froze. He could tell she didn't know how to handle it. He wasn't sure either, for that matter. He didn't want to lead her on. But he couldn't ignore his heart. Maybe there was a compromise to be found.

Madison eased back a little in her chair and avoided eye contact. Carsten moved away, too, giving her space. He remained kneeling by her chair, however, and removed the colored pencil from her hand. Setting it on the table, he turned and looked deep into her eyes.

"I know what you must be thinking."

Madison's eyes rounded.

"I know you're confused. I hope I haven't hurt you. I want you to know up front that I think about that night in Germany all the time. You've never been far from my mind ever since. You remained with me, Maddie."

Madison inhaled sharply. "Is that why you asked me to be your designer?"

Carsten hesitated. "Partly."

Madison raised an eyebrow in a silent question.

"And also because I believe God led us back to each other." He watched for a reaction, emotion welling up in his chest. It was true. If he believed God was involved in the good and the bad of life, he'd rather focus on the good. Like winning Maddie's heart so that once the danger was past, she might consider him.

Madison swallowed hard. "I'm glad," she finally whispered. She leaned forward to rest her forehead against his. "So where does that leave us?"

Carsten raised a finger to her lips to silence her question.

"We will wait and see, *mein engel*.."

~*~

Madison closed her eyes and reveled in the moment. Is this your will, Lord? Is he the one for me? The only answer her heart received was the repeat of Carsten's advice. *Wait.*

"We'll go shopping in the morning." Carsten rose to his feet and smiled down at her. "I might even buy you breakfast first." He winked and then slipped from the room.

Madison watched through the window as Carsten made his way back down to the stables. She smiled, thinking how well he fit in at the Running R. During the past few days, he had spent almost as much time with Samson as he did sleeping. He really loved that horse. She wondered if his new inheritance would bring him to the United States more often. Her heartbeat quickened at the thought.

She was staring into space, absently entertaining dreams of moving her lucrative business to Montana when Mitch appeared suddenly.

"I've been looking for you." He stood posed in the doorway, resting one elbow casually against the frame.

Madison began gathering her things, trying to

act casual. "I'm usually anywhere that's air conditioned." She faked a smile and stuffed a bunch of file folders into her tote bag. The foreman still made her uneasy, ever since that first day on the ranch during lunch. He was too brash, too bold, and something about his demeanor made Madison think he was used to getting everything he wanted. She had no intentions of becoming another check mark on his list.

"No need to run off." Mitch ambled into the room, settling into the chair beside her.

"I'm busy," Madison stated firmly. She finished filling her bag and started to stand up.

"But we haven't had a chance to get to know one another." He grabbed her chair before she could rise and pulled it closer toward him. Madison fell down hard in the seat and gasped in surprise.

She gathered her wits, fueled by anger and a touch of fear. "I have to go." She pushed her chair back firmly. It squeaked in protest.

"I don't think you understand." Mitch's voice lowered and he grabbed her wrist. "I just want to talk." The look in his eyes suggested otherwise.

Madison gave in to the surge of adrenaline and yanked her hand free. "Stay away from me!"

The front door slammed shut, and Mitch backed away.

"Madison, I forgot to tell you—" Carsten's voice trailed off as he took in the scene before him. "Is there a problem here?" His eyes darkened. Did he realize his accent grew stronger when he was upset? Madison watched his fist clench into a ball and knew she had to intervene. She cast a look at the foreman, who had pasted on an easy smile and was standing relaxed, hands in his pockets.

"No problem," she answered. She didn't want to cause drama on the ranch. The workers shouldn't have to deal with that kind of tension, and Carsten didn't need any more on his plate than he already had.

Mitch continued to smile. Carsten fixed him with a hard gaze and nodded. "I think you're needed in the stables." His tone left no room for arguing.

"Yes sir, boss." Mitch tipped his hat, just on the edge of sarcasm, and left the room.

Carsten focused on Madison. "Are you sure you're all right?"

"I'm sure." Madison felt her muscles relaxing. "He was just talking to me. No big deal."

"If you say so." Carsten still didn't look happy about the situation.

"I'm going to go call Shan back. I realized there are some things from the office I need shipped over for your project." Madison slung her tote on her shoulder and gave a quick wave as she passed him.

It wasn't until she was halfway up the stairs that she realized Carsten had never finished what he was saying when he had come back into the dining room.

12

The next morning, Madison rode into town with Carsten in the rental Jeep, the incident with Mitch forgotten. The tote bag at her feet was full of ideas and lists, and her stomach was full of pancakes with extra syrup from Molly's Diner.

Life was good.

"I know I'm going to gain at least ten pounds before I go back home." She grinned as she pushed a hand against her flat stomach.

"I doubt that." Carsten shot her an accessing glance before turning his attention back to the road. "If you do, it'll hardly hurt you."

Madison warmed at the compliment, ignoring the shame that came with having somewhat fished for it. Deciding it would be safer to shift into her work mode, she leaned forward and grabbed a three-ring binder from her bag.

"I think we should go to a paint store first." She opened the notebook and began flipping through the pages. "If you don't see anything you like for sure, then we'll bring home some samples and go from there."

"I told you, whatever you like is fine with me. I trust your professional opinion. I hired you, remember?" He grinned at her.

Madison flipped through the book of sketches in front of her. She had outlined some color schemes for the downstairs, and numbered them in the order of which she thought Carsten would like the best. She also planned to buy some things today in which to fix up her guest room. If she didn't get a mirror on the wall, stat, she might not survive the rest of her stay.

They parked in front of a supply store, and as they got out, Madison noticed several people shooting her curious looks. She glanced at Carsten. "Do I have syrup all over me or something?" She began brushing at the front of her designer dress trousers and fitted pink blouse.

"You look fine." Carsten assured her. "I think the locals aren't accustomed to seeing such…finery…in their small town."

Madison paused and glanced down at her silver jewelry and high heels. "Oh." She frowned and then looked at Carsten. She realized for the first time that he had worn wranglers and a work shirt every day since coming to the ranch.

"How do you do it?"

"Do what?"

"Fit in so easily, so quickly."

Carsten frowned, but it passed from his expression so quickly Madison wondered if she imagined it.

"I'm adaptable. Sort of like a chameleon." He flicked out his tongue, imitating a lizard, and Madison giggled.

"Well, this"—she dropped her gaze to her outfit—"is a problem that is easily fixed. Come on." She grabbed his arm and began pulling him down the sidewalk.

"Whoa, there. Where are you taking me?"

She winked. "To shop, of course. I noticed a Ladies Western Wear just down the street."

~*~

An hour later, Carsten sat waiting in a chair positioned outside the ladies' dressing room, tapping his boot in time to the country tune playing over the speakers. Years of following in his father's footsteps of detective work, and he hadn't seen this shopping spree coming. His skills must be slipping.

In the time they had been there, Madison had tried on what must have been the contents of at least half the store. The saleslady loved her—or more likely loved the money Madison was sure to spend—and kept bringing more outfits to her door.

Carsten had given up on trying to get a word in, and had resigned himself to waiting for the inevitable. Eventually, she would have nothing left to try on, and then they could continue their original plan of shopping for supplies.

The door to the dressing room swung open, and Carsten turned his attention to Madison. She stepped outside in a pair of dark denim jeans and a long sleeve western blouse.

"What do you think?" She did a little spin in front of the three-way mirror.

He grinned and repeated what he had said about every outfit before. "It looks nice." And it did. With her blonde hair and fair complexion, she could be a model even if she wore a burlap sack.

She planted her hands on her hips and huffed. "You said that already."

He eased his arms back behind his head in a casual pose. "I'm telling the truth each time."

Madison rolled her eyes and went back inside the dressing room.

"You're no help," she hollered over the door. He saw her feet stomp below the door as she stepped out of the jeans. He averted his gaze. Those thoughts would quickly lead him nowhere.

"How are we doing?" The saleslady cooed. She looked elated. No doubt, she was imagining her commission from the impending sale.

"Fine." Carsten and Madison replied at the same time. The saleslady shot Carsten a look.

"I was talking to the missus." She fixed him with a sharp gaze then headed back to the register.

Carsten glanced at his watch, thought it was nearing lunchtime, and leaned back until his chair was resting on two legs. He rocked aimlessly; keeping the chair balanced as he tried to think of a place nearby where they could eat.

The dressing room door opened again, and Madison stepped out in a black dress. He took one look and lost his balance, toppling onto his back as the chair tipped over underneath him.

Carsten did a quick backwards roll and came easily to his feet, clearing his throat. He struck a quick, relaxed pose, hands in his pockets, as if nothing had happened.

"That's nice, too." His conscious screamed at him. *Liar!*

Madison looked gorgeous. He couldn't take his eyes off her. Her pale skin appeared porcelain under the modest, but extremely flattering cut of the dress.

She stepped hesitantly to the mirror. "Are you sure?" She turned to check out the back view.

Carsten stopped his eyes from following with

will power he didn't know he possessed. "Oh, I'm sure." His voice was husky, and Madison shot him a surprised look in the mirror.

He dropped his gaze, and took the opportunity to straighten the chair.

"I think I'm done." Madison observed him from the corner of her eye. He still wouldn't look at her. "And I think I'm getting this dress."

Carsten looked up. "You do, and I'll be forced to take you out to dinner tomorrow night."

Madison gave him a sassy smile as she stepped back inside the dressing room. "There are worse fates." She shut the door behind her.

~*~

"I really like the blue." Carsten pointed to the sample in Madison's right hand.

She shook the sample in her left. "But what about the accent color? Which shade of yellow?"

"The top one."

"Sunset yellow? Are you crazy? It's so gold!"

"Fine. The bottom one, then."

"Corn silk? It might as well be white!"

Carsten ran a hand through his hair and took a deep breath.

"Madison?"

"Hmmm?" She was still preoccupied with holding samples up to her sketches.

"Why do you ask my opinion if you argue with it every time?"

She looked up, startled.

"Am I doing that? I'm sorry." She sighed and rolled her neck around on her shoulders. "I get tense when I'm doing a big project. I want everything to look perfect. Shan tells me all the time that I need to relax and let the design speak for itself."

Carsten gently began massaging her neck and shoulders. "I understand that. I just don't like being constantly shot down. I've told you before, I really don't care what you choose."

Madison made a moaning noise in the back of her throat, and Carsten assumed the massage was helping. He kept going.

"If you ask my opinion, I'll gladly give it, but if you're not really willing to use the answer that I give, then save yourself the trouble and decide for yourself."

Madison opened her eyes. "I can do that."

She pulled a few more samples from the rack in front of her, and then turned suddenly to face Carsten. "I have an idea."

Carsten raised his eyebrows.

"Why don't you leave me to picking out the rest of this stuff, and go grab us a table next door at the café? I'll be done soon, and you can sit and get some coffee while you wait on me. I know you're probably sick of looking at all of this."

Carsten hesitated. He didn't want to leave her alone for very long. He shot a glance over his shoulder. Surely a few minutes couldn't hurt? But what if they were being followed, and a few minutes was all the culprit was waiting for? He frowned.

"I'll be fine," Madison insisted. She began pushing him toward the door. "Go on."

Carsten gave in, but only half way. He stepped outside and waited until he saw Madison go back to the selection of paint supplies. Then he jogged to the café, requested a table be put on hold, and returned to the storefront. He watched her from outside the window as she continued her shopping.

Madison looked completely carefree as she selected item after item for her shopping cart. She appeared unaware, or perhaps just undaunted, by her current circumstances. Carsten found that fact both comforting and cause for alarm. He wanted her to stay alert so she could help to protect herself. But at the same time, he wanted her to be lighthearted and joyful. She didn't need to know the truth, because nothing was going to hurt her. Not while she was on his watch.

13

When Madison arrived back at the ranch, she found an overnight express package sitting on her bed. Rita had probably delivered it to the room for her. She studied the label and realized that Shan had sent the items from the office.

Madison eagerly tore into the packaging, pulling out packs of colored pencils, a new sketchpad, several design magazines, and her favorite fabric swatches. She picked up the color wheel and spun it on her finger, feeling her creative muse return. She couldn't wait to start bringing the paper sketches to life inside the house.

Madison glanced into the box and felt around in the tissue paper, checking to see if she had missed anything. Her hand brushed against something soft, and she pulled it out of the box. It was her new stuffed angel with a note pinned to the front.

She read the note and laughed.

Madison—I thought you might need a friend while you were away from home. I wasn't sure which was your favorite, so I chose the newest one. Hope I made the right choice! Have fun and be careful—Love Shan

P.S. Don't do anything I wouldn't do!

Madison smiled. Only Shan.

She smoothed back the angel's fluffy wings. Once again, she was reminded of her favorite place, her favorite moment. She studied the face of the doll. It was funny how something so commonplace for most people could completely transport her to another time.

She hugged the angel against her body and then nestled it against the pillows on the bed in a place of honor. Looking around the small room, she decided this was as good a time as any to get started on decorating.

"Might as well spruce up my own room first." Madison caught herself talking out loud and shook her head in amusement. She had definitely been on the ranch too long. But her absence from the city didn't necessarily feel like a negative thing. What would it be like to return? Would she fit right back in? Or would a country twang accent her words, like was beginning to tinge Carsten's voice? Would she come to prefer her new straight legged jeans and boots to the pencil skirts and heels that filled her closet at home? Only time would tell.

The next few hours were a blur of activity as Madison worked her magic on the bedroom. First, she changed the sheets; replacing them with ones she had bought earlier that afternoon. Decorative throw pillows were placed strategically on the bed, and then she hung curtains at the window, and nailed pictures on the walls.

She plugged in the new lamp on top of the nightstand and smiled at the effect. Much improved. She cast a look around the transformed guest room.

The blinding white accessories from before had been changed into a palette of color. The bed featured pastel polka dots in shades of green and purple, with yellow accent pillows. The curtains were sheer lavender and blew gently in the breeze from the open window. Framed flower boxes hung in an arrangement over the bed, creating a new focal point. The soft lighting changed the entire atmosphere of the room, making the small space appear cozy, rather than cramped.

Madison turned at a knock on the door. Rita stepped inside, holding a dishtowel and smelling of fresh rolls. Flour was streaked across the front of the apron tied around her waist. Her face carried an expression of delight and surprise.

"Well I never!" Rita's eyes roamed around the guest room. "Will you just take a look at that!"

"I hope it's OK." She looked to the older woman anxiously. Although Madison didn't really know Rita, her opinion mattered.

"It's beautiful, child!" Rita walked inside the room and turned a slow circle. "I've never been the type that enjoys doing all this girlie hub-bug, but that doesn't mean I can't appreciate the results! You did a nice job."

Madison smoothed the wrinkles from the quilt. "Thank you, Rita."

"I can't wait to see what you do with the rest of this house."

Madison grinned. "Me either. My ideas are still a bit…here and there. My final choices haven't quite come together yet. But we made great progress shopping today."

With her foot, she tapped the box that had been delivered from New York. "And hopefully, this will give me new incentive. My partner sent me some of my things from the office."

"I wondered what was in that big ol' box! Well, I'm sure you'll do just fine, honey, whatever you decide. Anything done to this house will be an improvement." Rita waved the dishtowel dramatically.

The housekeeper turned to leave, then paused and caught Madison's eye. "I bet our favorite German will be very impressed." She winked and left the room.

Madison sat on the edge of the bed, feeling a blush creep up her neck. Were her feelings for Carsten so obvious that even Rita noticed? Madison's gaze wandered to the stuffed angel, and she once again remembered the feel of Carsten's lips upon hers. A delightful shiver skittered through her.

The shrill ring of her cellphone interrupted her thoughts. Madison plucked the phone from her purse and glanced at the caller I.D. It was Shan.

"Hey girlfriend, what's up?"

"Madison…it happened again."

Madison's carefree attitude disappeared and she sat bolt upright at the sound of fear in Shan's voice. "What do you mean?"

"They ransacked the office."

Madison closed her eyes briefly. "Are you OK?"

"Yes…no…I don't know. I'm freaked out." Shan's voice shook.

Madison leaned forward on the bed. "It's going to be fine." *Maybe.* She didn't really believe her own words. "Did they take anything?"

"I don't think so. It's hard to tell. I can't really think straight."

"Are you safe?"

"Yes. The police just left. I'm on my way back home."

Madison sighed in relief. "What happened?" Her gaze automatically darted to the window, but she forced away the paranoia. She was thousands of miles from New York. She was safe.

But was Shan? And what about their hard work in the office? Insurance would have to be filed…what a nightmare.

"I closed up the office at 6:00, same as usual. I got home and fixed dinner, then realized that I had left my portfolio in your office. I really needed it to prepare for meeting with the Andersons tomorrow, so I went back to get it. I think it was around 9:30. "

Madison glanced at her watch. It read 8:45 p.m. Shan was two hours ahead with the time difference.

"Whoever did it was good, Madison. The front door didn't show any signs of being forced open, but it wasn't locked. I thought maybe I had forgotten to lock it on my way out. Once I saw your office, I realized that wasn't true. It was a wreck, a complete wreck."

"Was anything destroyed?" Madison held her breath.

Shan sighed deeply. "I don't think so. Our supplies were left alone. The desk drawers were pulled out, and all the cabinet doors were hung open. But nothing seemed stolen or broken."

Relief flooded. Then confusion. "That's odd. Why bother, then?" Madison's brow knitted and her heart skipped a beat. The same thing had happened at her apartment. No reason, no motive…just disaster.

Malice.

"I don't know, but the weird part was your angel collection. The dolls were scattered all over the office. Almost as if someone had picked up and discarded each one."

Madison's eyes widened. "Are they broken?"

"No, they're fine. After the police left, I straightened them back up for you. I know how much you love those things. They seem to all be there, but it's hard to tell. There's so many of them." Shan laughed, but it sounded forced.

"Thank you for doing that." Madison collapsed against the pillows in relief. "This is really getting strange."

"You're telling me!" Shan's usual fire began to return. "I'm about ready to get to this bottom of this! People just don't have the right to be breaking into other people's places and messing up stuff for no reason."

"I'd almost rather have had them rob me," Madison admitted. "At least then I would know and understand the motive. Who breaks into a place and leaves all the expensive stuff?" She shivered. Someone with something other than burglary on their minds. What did they want? What could she possibly have?

"I don't know, girl, but I sure hope the police figure it out. They didn't seem to have much hope when they left here."

"They said the same thing when they were at my apartment. This criminal must not be leaving behind any clues."

"Smart guy."

Madison grimaced. "That just makes it scarier."

14

As soon as Madison disconnected the call, she hurried from the guestroom and rushed down the stairs to the kitchen. "Carsten!"

"I think he's asleep, honey." Rita shut the refrigerator door. "Do you need something?"

"I need to talk with him. Right now! It's urgent." Pulse pounding, Madison jogged down the hall to Carsten's room. His door was shut. She knocked twice and then entered without thinking.

"Carsten!" She came to a sudden stop in the middle of the room.

He jerked awake. "Madison? Are you all right?" He flung back the covers, and then seemed to realize too late that he was clad only in his boxer shorts. He tugged the sheets back into place.

Madison ducked her head, avoiding his gaze. Yet somehow, her traitorous eyes kept darting back to the sight of him, shirtless under the quilt.

"I—I need to talk." She stammered over the words, feeling like a bigger idiot with each passing second. "I'm sorry I woke you up." Her face burned.

"Not a problem, Maddie." Carsten rubbed his eyes with his fist, but made no move to get up. "I'll be right there."

His accent was thicker when he was awakened, too. It did funny things to her insides. What would it be like to hear his voice that way each morning? She swayed on her feet and then suddenly realized she was still standing in the middle of his bedroom. "Oh! Sorry!" She quickly ducked back into the hall, pulling the door shut behind her. *You idiot!*

But, no matter how many names she called herself; she couldn't stop remembering how adorable he looked while sleeping.

~*~

Carsten joined Madison within minutes, dressed in jeans and a sweatshirt. He pushed back his hair and took her arm. "Let's go to the porch. The fresh air will do both of us some good." He led her outside to the swing. "What's wrong?"

Madison took a deep breath. She leaned back against the swing and pushed off with her feet, rocking in a slow rhythm. "Shan just called. The office was broken into."

"What?" Carsten turned to face her abruptly, setting the swing off balance.

Madison grabbed the chain to steady herself. "My reaction was about the same."

Carsten set the swing back into motion as Madison explained the details of the phone call.

"This is real, isn't it?" she whispered. "I think it's just now sinking in."

"Come here." Carsten raised his arm and tucked her against him. "It's going to be all right. You're safe with me, *fraulein*."

Madison relaxed against him. He leaned down and imbibed the clean scent of her hair. She smelled like wildflowers. He closed his eyes. He could stay here forever.

She eased away slightly, but didn't disentangle

herself from his embrace completely. "I hate feeling like this, Carsten. Helpless. Out of control. My faith should be stronger than what it is. I should be able to trust that God has everything in hand."

Carsten opened his eyes, not sure what to say. Who was he to give advice on faith? His was as shaky as it got. He smoothed a piece of Madison's hair from her face, reveling in its softness. He felt the urge to pray, but he wasn't sure what to say, wasn't sure what he needed. He glanced down at the angel in his arms. He knew what he wanted, that was for certain.

"I think you are very strong, Maddie. You've handled this well. It's normal to feel a little out of control right now." Despite her occasional bursts of anxiety, she'd handled well all the upheaval in her life. Many of his clients over the years had coped with lesser situations with considerably less class.

She sighed and snuggled closer against his shoulder. He tried to refocus his thoughts. What did Madison need? What was in her best interest? Keeping her safe, of course, but also keeping her spirits up. She was indeed a strong woman; it showed it every aspect of her life. Sometimes the panic seeped in through the cracks, but her overall confidence was high. Carsten suspected that was because of her faith, despite her fears that it was lacking. She had a more solid foundation than most women her age. It was intriguing.

He decided the best thing to do for both of them would be to go on with their date for the next night as planned. The temporary escape would distract Madison and keep her creative mind focused for her current design project. The best thing for her would be to just keep going. Forge ahead and not let the evil win. Meanwhile, he'd make some calls to his home office and discuss a plan of action with his team. He needed someone with eyes in New York while they were here in Montana. He needed clues to work with, a solid lead—and fast.

Several minutes passed as the pair sat swinging on the porch, enjoying the cool night air and each other's warmth. But Carsten's eyes searched the darkness, always alert. He never stopped watching. However far away, the danger was real.

He wouldn't forget that.

15

Madison sprayed a fine mist of her favorite perfume on her neck and then allowed another glance in the mirror she had installed on the back of the bedroom door. She inhaled deeply in a feeble attempt to settle her stomach.

"It's just a date," she told her reflection. "Not even really an official date. More like an opportunity to wear a new dress." But if that were true, then why didn't her heart believe it? And why was her stomach jumping at the prospect of spending time with Carsten in their first date-like environment?

Pushing the thoughts aside, she did a little twirl in front of the mirror, and smiled with satisfaction. She looked nice. Strange how out of all the expensive outfits she had possessed during her lifetime, she found her favorite one hiding in a western store in a tiny, forgotten town.

Madison clasped a string of pearls around her neck, took a deep breath, and stepped back from the mirror. No more procrastination. It was time to face Carsten, butterflies or not. She couldn't wait to see the look on his face when he saw her dressed up again.

She wasn't let down. Madison caught a glimpse of Carsten's expression as she carefully descended the stairs in her black high-heels.

"*Mensch*," he breathed, reaching out to steady

her as she took the last step.

She raised her face to his questioningly. Was that good or bad?

"Wow," he translated.

Madison fought the blush she felt rise to her ears. Carsten looked nice, too, in a dark suit and white dress shirt. His tie held flecks of pale blue that brought his eyes to life. They sparkled as he gazed down on her, and her heart leapt into her throat.

"Thank you," she responded. She shifted awkwardly. As much as she was enjoying her role in this acted-out fairytale, she was eager to regain their usual level of comfort with each other.

"Shall we?" Carsten extended his arm with a slight bow.

Grinning, she allowed him to lead her outside to the car. She saw the blinds snap close as they passed the window. Rita was spying.

As soon as they were both settled in the Jeep, she turned to Carsten with a smile. "Do you feel like you're thirteen again and this is your first date?"

They laughed together, and the previous awkwardness fled.

"I should have known Rita would want to spy." Carsten shifted the Jeep into gear and began the trek down the long gravel drive. "She's a perpetual matchmaker."

Carsten buckled his seatbelt. "I thought we'd try the seafood restaurant downtown. It's the most formal this county has."

"You mean this place has a downtown?" He laughed. "Yes, and you already saw it. It was where we went shopping. Don't tell me you miss the big city already?"

Now she was the one to shrug. Did she? "Parts of it, maybe."

They rode in amiable silence during the drive into town, and parked in front of Gill's Seafood.

"Gill's?" Madison raised an eyebrow as Carsten helped her out of the car. The name sounded more like a surf shack on a beachfront tourist trap than a formal restaurant.

"It's nicer inside than it sounds."

And it was. Madison was impressed. It was no Tavern on the Green, but it was considerably upscale considering they were basically in the middle of nowhere.

"Do you live in luxury in Germany, or is the small-town atmosphere more your taste? What are you accustomed to?" Madison leaned forward, slipping her menu on the edge of the table. She already knew she wanted the lobster.

"That's a good question." Carsten laid his menu on top of hers and reached for his water glass. "I travel a lot. I'm not always in Germany." He tilted his head. "I suppose I'm not really accustomed to anything."

She frowned, noticing again his lack of answer to a direct question. She opened her mouth to press further, but Carsten beat her to it.

"What about you, Maddie?" He narrowed his eyes. "Do you prefer mountains and streams to the skyscrapers and the concrete jungle, as they say?"

Madison paused. "Actually…" She hedged. She wanted to answer; she didn't want to make him feel as though she were avoiding the question, as he had done to her. But the truth was, she really wasn't sure. She felt one way in the city, another in the country. Almost as if her personality was split in half. Not to mention her discontent in New York had been building long before Carsten reappeared in her life.

"Maybe I'm a contradiction." She laid her napkin in her lap and smoothed the edges. Having been gone this long, she did miss the shopping and the restaurants and the coffee shops New York offered? "A part of me appreciates the beauty of the; the other part thrives on the opportunities of the city."

"And which side dominates?" Carsten leaned forward as if her answers mattered greatly.

"Salad and breadsticks!" The waiter eased the appetizers down on the table, interrupting the moment. "Fresh ground pepper?"

At Madison's nod, Carsten indicated for the man to grind the mill.

"Thank you." He turned back to Madison, but the moment had passed.

Madison fought the temptation to squirm under Carsten's intense gaze. How could he look at her like that and appear to be reading her every thought? Or worse, how he could possibly want to know her every thought? She wasn't used to this much attention. Not sincere attention, anyway. She bit into the breadstick. The delicious garlic flavor distracted her, and she took another bite.

"This is a really nice place." She smiled. "Thank you for bringing me here."

Carsten scooted a tomato to the edge of his plate with his fork. "You're very welcome, Maddie." He looked like he wanted to say more, but he remained silent.

Madison watched as he moved aside a piece of bell pepper before taking a bite of the salad. She grinned at her sudden discovery. "You're a picky eater, aren't you?"

Carsten ducked his head, not replying due to the food in his mouth, and just shrugged. He grinned.

Madison smirked. Her prince wasn't perfect after all. The thought put her strangely at ease.

The lobster was delicious, as was the half-cup of clam chowder that accompanied it. She leaned back in her chair. "I'm too full to move. I think that ten pounds I keep talking about gaining is finally here."

Leaning back in his chair as well, Carsten edged his almost empty plate of crab legs further from him. "You still look beautiful. But I feel the same way."

"Dessert?" The waiter appeared at the table with a dessert tray, piled high with an assortment of incredibly delicious, incredibly fattening choices.

"Mmm, is that cheesecake?" Madison pointed to the item closest to her.

Carsten threw his head back and laughed. "Too full to move, you say?"

Madison shrugged sheepishly.

Carsten turned to the waiter. "I believe we'll take a piece of cheesecake."

The waiter nodded and moved away.

"I found an unoccupied spot." Madison lifted her chin and moved aside her plate to make room for its coming replacement. "If you're nice, I'll share." She winked.

"Oh will you, now? Seems only fair since I'm picking up the check."

The teasing banter went on until the piece of cake was delivered. The waiter set the plate closest to Madison, and she stuck her tongue out at Carsten in victory.

Some time later, all that remained on the table were the crumbs from the cake crust and the wad of bills that Carsten placed on the check.

"Ready to go, or will you need a wheelbarrow for assistance?" Carsten stood and reached his hand out to Madison.

She rose purposefully on her own and picked up her purse, wrinkling her nose at him. "I'll do just fine, thank you very much." But she wanted to be close. She wrapped her arm through his and nestled against his side as they exited the restaurant. Did the evening have to end?

"I hope you enjoyed dinner." Carsten turned to her as they stepped into the lobby, untucking her hand from his arm and trailing his fingers down to her wrist. An eager expression shone in his eyes that reminded Madison of a boy with his first love.

Was it love? She swallowed hard, and hoped her gaze didn't mimic Carsten's too closely. It was getting harder to hide her feelings from him. She was afraid to make the first move. But did she want to? It was her turn. After all, Carsten had put his heart on the line during that whispered confession in the dining room. Madison tightened her grip on her fingers. She was hesitant to move too fast. It was wise to move slowly, seek God's will, and wait to see what happened. Or was that presumptuous? Did God care about her love life, or did He expect her to make the right decisions on her own?

"I had a great time." Madison smiled her appreciation. Deep thoughts could wait. For now, she'd just enjoy the moment.

Carsten pushed open the front door. The sudden rain shower took them both by surprise, and Carsten hurried to settle Madison into the passenger seat of the Jeep. She locked the door and leaned against it, brushing back her damp hair as she watched Carsten jog around the front to the driver's side. She stared at him when he sat down, shaking water from his hair.

"What?" He questioned, freezing in place. "Is something wrong?" A raindrop trickled down the side of his face and dripped off his chin.

Just that he looked incredibly kissable…

Madison turned off the thought and shook her head. "Not a thing." She smiled. "Just thinking." Was the slight stubble of whiskers on his chin as rough as it looked? Or surprisingly soft? She yearned to find out. But her heart screamed caution.

Carsten furrowed his brow but didn't comment as he began backing the Jeep out of the parking space.

The rain continued steadily as they drove back toward the ranch. Suddenly, Carsten pulled the car to the side of the road.

Her heartbeat increased. "What are you doing? What's wrong?" Madison sat up and looked around. Had he seen something? Was her stalker out there? She couldn't see anything through the driving rain.

Carsten didn't answer, and her stomach twisted. This must be bad. He got out of the Jeep. Then he smiled, and Madison relaxed. No danger. But what was he up to?

He hurried around to her door and opened it. Madison squealed and edged away from the water streaming down the lining of the car. She looked up at him in confusion.

"Would you like to dance?" He offered his hand.

Madison gaped at him. Is he serious?

"It's raining," she protested. Carsten remained still, hand outstretched, waiting.

Silly girl…

She put her hand in his.

They danced, the headlights from the car shining a spotlight through the rain.

Madison ignored the fact that her new dress was getting soaked. She didn't think about the fact that she was standing in a puddle. She didn't notice the way the water from her hair streamed down her face, ruining her carefully constructed makeup.

The only thing existing in the world was the two of them, dancing together without music, listening only to the way their hearts beat together as one, echoing the steady pounding of rain on the roof of the Jeep. They danced, on and on, just as they had that magical night so many years before.

16

Madison sat silently in the Jeep, listening to the thunder rumble as they drove back to the ranch. The interior of the car was soaked and she was shivering on the outside, but her heart was so warm she didn't care.

Neither had spoken a word since Carsten's invitation to dance, but much had been said, just the same. Sometimes thoughts were best expressed without words.

Carsten reached to the console and turned the dial to activate the heater. The floorboards warmed instantly, and Madison pushed off her wet shoes, wiggling her damp toes against the flow of air.

She tried to analyze what was in her heart. *God*? She wanted His opinion. Was He watching, listening? Madison closed her eyes. Carsten hummed softly. What had just taken place?

They had shared a dance, true, but so much more than just that. It had felt like an unspoken agreement of the heart. They had forged a bond, an unexplainable, undeniable connection that linked their souls together. It first happened that night in Germany, and had maintained its strength over a stretch of time and distance. Was this what love felt like? Madison wasn't sure, but she knew she didn't want the feeling to go away.

Her musings made the drive back pass quickly.

She exited the car, feeling as if she were floating on air, cliché as the expression might be. She hardly noticed the way her wet shoes rubbed a blister on her little toe. She noticed nothing but the delicious way she felt inside. Was this what home felt like? Was that what she'd been missing all these years?

Carsten took Madison's hand as she reached to open the front door. She paused and then made her decision. She tilted her face up to his. His lips covered hers in a gentle, sweet kiss.

Madison's heartbeat increased. When he kissed her, he really kissed her. There was nothing else like it. Carsten nuzzled her cheek with his. It wasn't rough at all, but smooth and intoxicating. She kissed him again. Carsten slowly backed away.

"We better go inside," he said firmly. His voice was deep, and Madison knew the reserved look in his eyes. It meant they needed to go inside and have Rita act as chaperone. She warmed at his chivalry, and despite the flutter of disappointment, she nodded.

Carsten opened the door and led the way inside. He bent down and kissed Madison on the forehead. "Go on to bed. We'll talk tomorrow." His eyes said everything his words didn't.

Madison obeyed, feeling as if each stair under her feet was the next stepping-stone to the fulfillment of her dreams. Who would have thought after all this time, she and Carsten would find a way back to each other? *Thank you, God. Maybe this really was You all along.*

Humming softly, Madison flipped on the light to her room. She froze in the doorway. Something was different. Heart pounding in her temples, she sucked in a breath of air. All instincts screamed to run, but she fought against it. What was giving her this feeling? There was no obvious danger. Yet everything felt wrong.

Braced against the doorframe, she scanned her belongings. What had she seen as she had stepped inside that caused her so much alarm? Her gaze roamed over the nightstand. Everything seemed normal there. The scarf she had picked up while dressing and then discarded was still lying on top of the dresser beside her arrangement of perfumes and other toiletries.

She tried thinking about the room in a professional sense. That's when she saw it. The framed pictures of the flowers above the bed weren't as she had originally hung them. She'd put the purple one closest to the window. Hadn't she?

She blinked, suddenly not as certain. Ridiculous. Why would someone rearrange her artwork?

Madison brushed off the nervous feeling, and began removing her jewelry. Maybe Rita had been upstairs earlier, and switched the pictures around. Even as she thought it, Madison dismissed the idea. Rita didn't care about artwork or anything decorative. Why would she move her things around? It didn't make sense, as much as she wanted it to.

Still thinking, she laid her bracelet and earrings on top of the dresser next to her hairbrush, and then reached back and started to unzip her dress.

Madison froze and then pushed a hand against her mouth to ward off the impending shriek. She distinctly remembered thinking earlier that it was time for her to clean out her brush again. The hairbrush lying on the dresser was free of hair.

"Carsten!" She screamed as she fled the room and began descending the stairs, her damp dress flapping open in the back as she ran. "Carsten!"

He sprang out of the kitchen at her cry, and took the stairs two at a time to meet her. He grabbed her arms. "What's wrong? Is someone there?" He pushed her against the wall out of his way and continued climbing before he received an answer, his hand already on the gun he had tucked into the back of his dress pants.

Madison's eyes rounded. Since when does he carry a gun?

Suddenly, nothing made sense. The room spun. She sank to a sitting position on the stairs. Was this a dream? The whole mood of the night was ruined. There were too many questions. And no answers.

She stared aimlessly as water dripped from the ends of her hair, forming a tiny puddle on her knee. Her fairytale had just taken a horrible turn.

Carsten. With a gun. She closed her eyes.

"What's going on?"

Madison opened her eyes to see Rita hurrying down the hall from the direction of her bedroom. She came to an abrupt stop in the living room. "I thought I heard someone running…" She saw Madison crouched on the stairs, and rushed over to join her. "Are you hurt?" She seemed to notice Madison's dress was halfway unzipped, and she frowned. "Are you—" Her voice trailed off.

"I got scared upstairs." Madison's lips turned up in a humorless half-smile. "Carsten is checking things out." *With a gun.* She kept that thought to herself.

Something hardened in Rita's eyes, but before Madison could define it, Rita reached for her dress. "I'll fix that for you." She zipped up the back in a brisk motion. "There you go."

"Thank you."

Carsten appeared at the top of the stairs. "Everything is fine," he announced with a hint of frustration. "What happened?" He tucked the revolver back behind him and crossed his arms over his chest.

Madison looked down at her hands. What was she supposed to say? *Someone broke into the house, rearranged my artwork and cleaned my personal grooming items?* Had she imagined the entire thing?

"I must have misunderstood." She rose slowly to her feet. "I'm sorry," she continued stiffly.

"Maddie," Carsten coaxed. "It's all right to tell me what scared you. I want you to be safe. If something happened, anything at all that made you uneasy, I need to know what that was."

Madison shrugged, more than a little embarrassed. "Something just felt off." She closed her eyes against the memory of the panicky feeling. "I thought maybe my pictures were switched around."

Carsten raised an eyebrow. "Is that all?" Relief rushed over his features.

"Well, that, and my hairbrush was clean. I remember it being full of hair earlier. I know that's gross, but I remember thinking that I needed to clean it out, but hadn't gotten to it yet."

Carsten exchanged a look with Rita, his face tense. "Why don't you ladies go to the kitchen and I'll join you in a bit." It was a command, not a suggestion. Madison had never heard him use that tone. She was more than willing to get away from it. She moved quickly down the stairs, Rita at her heels. What was going on? Did Rita have any answers? She knew something. That much was obvious.

Madison decided to use the time alone to question the older woman. She somehow always seemed to know exactly what was going on around the ranch. Madison was surprised that Rita hadn't noticed anything odd upstairs earlier in the evening.

Or had she?

"Were you home the whole time that Carsten and I were out?" Madison tried to keep her voice sounding relaxed, even while her body tensed tighter and tighter. She hid her clenched fists in her lap.

Rita pulled out the barstool next to Madison, handing her a clean dishrag. "You might want to dry off a little. You must be freezing." She cleared her throat. "Yes, I was home tonight, but I was in my room most of the evening. I took a bath, and then began watching a movie on television. I think I dozed off for a little while. I never heard a thing from upstairs."

Madison frowned, squeezing the dampness from her hair with the towel. "Maybe my imagination was just running wild. I could have been mistaken. Maybe I did move the picture and clean my brush, and I just don't remember."

Rita kept silent, an unusual decision for the outgoing woman. She looked as if she was trying her best not to say something.

Madison pursed her lips and tossed the rag onto the counter. "Are you—"She was interrupted by

Carsten entering the kitchen.

"I'm almost through checking the house. I wanted to make sure you were all right." The words were spoken to both of them, but his eyes stared straight into Madison's. She ducked her head, still unsure of how she was feeling. That gun had changed so many things. She'd realized this was a ranch, but wouldn't that mean shotguns and rifles? Not pistols.

What else did she not know about Carsten?

She needed answers. Now. She turned back to Rita.

"How about some tea?" Rita put on a bright smile and began rummaging through the pantry. "That will calm us right down. I do love a good cup of strong tea when I need to relax." She turned on the faucet to fill the kettle as Carsten exited the room.

"Rita." Madison leaned forward, resting her elbows against the counter, trying to get the woman's attention.

Rita glanced over her shoulder and then pretended not to have heard.

"Rita!" Madison didn't mean to raise her voice, but her patience was rapidly approaching its limit.

"Oh, all right." Rita turned on the fire under the kettle and faced Madison with a huff. "I do know more than I'm saying, and what I am saying is that you need to talk to Carsten before you hear anything from me. And that's all I'm gonna say." She took a deep breath.

Madison couldn't help but grin at Rita speaking so flustered. "I'm sorry to push. I just hate secrets."

Rita mumbled something under her breath, and

Madison decided this wasn't the best time to ask her to repeat it.

She needed at least one answer. "Why was he carrying a gun?" Madison lowered her voice. Carsten might be within earshot. But Rita kept her back to Madison, and didn't answer. Was that part of what she refused to discuss? Madison blew out a frustrated breath. Had everyone gone crazy?

Carsten came back inside the kitchen, squelching her vain attempts to gather information. "We're clear," he stated. He dropped onto the vacated barstool beside Madison and leaned on top of the counter, resting his face in his palms. He rubbed his hands roughly across his forehead, and then lifted his gaze to meet that of the women.

"Tea?" Rita held up a glass, her answer to the world's problems.

Carsten shook his head. "I suppose we should talk." His gaze met Madison's gravely.

"Living room?" He stood and gestured in the direction of the den. Madison followed reluctantly.

Just minutes ago, she was practically floating, feeling free as a bird and certain her destiny had caught up with her. Now, each step felt as if she were edging closer to the gallows. Not toward her own death, but rather to the death of the relationship forming so delicately between her and Carsten.

17

Madison sank into the corner of the couch and tucked her feet underneath her. She was still wearing the dress she had gone out in, and she tugged at the hem to cover her knees. The magic of the dress, and the whole evening, had disappeared. All that lingered was the remnants of fear and the imminent sense of peril that Madison couldn't shake.

Carsten reached over and draped a down blanket over her shoulders. This time, his touch didn't bring the measure of safety it usually did. He must have sensed it too, because he moved to sit on the hearth of the fireplace, rather than on the couch near her.

She couldn't decide if that bothered her.

"Are you all right, Maddie?"

The question was so soft that Madison wasn't even certain he had asked it. He appeared to be waiting for a response, though. "I'm fine. I mean, physically, I'm OK." She adjusted the blanket, wrapping it more securely around her body, wishing it could do a better job of hiding her.

"But not emotionally." Carsten finished her thought. He sighed. "That's my fault. I know you saw the gun. I am sorry about that."

Madison nodded, not trusting the words that might slip out. She didn't like guns. Although she'd never had a bad experience with one, she'd never felt comfortable in their presence. But Carsten couldn't have known that, and she didn't blame him for it—especially if he had been attempting to protect her from all this madness.

But the question of why he had a gun still remained, and lurked like an elephant in the corner of the room

"I like to be prepared," Carsten began slowly, as if choosing his words carefully, too.

Why would he need to if he wasn't hiding something? Madison squeezed her eyes shut. She hated the level of distrust she now had toward Carsten. How much did she really know about this man, anyway?

Except that he was ridiculously romantic and an amazing kisser. Facts that were great by moonlight but not so much in the stark light of reality

"I didn't realize it would bother you so much," he continued. "Now, I know. I'll make sure you don't see it again."

"Then that means you plan on carrying it again." Madison couldn't hide the frustration in her voice, even though she couldn't fully understand where it was coming from. Was the gun really the issue here?

She was afraid to answer that, afraid of what probing deeper would mean—even to herself.

Carsten took a deep breath. "Madison, I have to keep you safe. You're aware that things weren't at their best when you left New York. I just want to be ready in case the worst were to happen."

"But it was in your suit pants! Did you have it with you throughout our entire date?" She swallowed against the lump in her throat, hating the sharp edge of her tone but unable to rein it in. None of this made sense.

"Yes, I did. I keep it with me at all times."

It wasn't about the gun. She couldn't deny it anymore. The gun she could adjust to.

It was how it had changed Carsten right before her eyes that she couldn't reconcile with. She didn't know him anymore.

Silence strained between them.

Then Carsten's previous words sank in and Madison narrowed her eyes. "What do you mean by 'the worst'? What do you think is going to happen out here?" She raised her chin, refusing to let the panic show. But her hands grew sweaty, and she gripped the blanket tighter. "I thought you said coming here would make me safe."

Even as the words left her mouth, she realized the truth. There was no safe. Safe was an illusion.

He stood and began to pace in front of the fireplace. "I didn't want to ever have this conversation." His own frustration was evident. "But maybe you should know the truth."

"Yeah, maybe I should." The sarcasm was a better blanket to hide behind than the down one covering her shoulders. She shrugged out of it, her anger warming her more thoroughly than the quilt ever could.

If she could just stay angry, maybe the hurt would keep its distance.

Carsten paused, bracing one arm against the mantle. Her stomach pitched.. What could possibly be that bad? What didn't she know?

In a sudden rush of words, the truth emerged.

"Your father called and hired me to protect you the night of the break-in at your apartment. I'm your official guardian, Madison."

The room dipped; Carsten's words swirled between them but refused to land long enough to comprehend. She reached desperately for one. Protect. Guardian? Her *dad*? How did he know her dad?

"I—I don't understand." Madison hated herself for stammering. She needed control. She needed to be in charge. She squared her shoulders but the helplessness of the situation threatened to overwhelm her.

Anxious, she clung to the remnants of her anger, fanning the flames afresh. Her father had hired Carsten?

"*Hired* you? You mean, all of this—" She gestured between them. It was fake. And his feelings for her...

A knot settled in her throat and refused to budge "All of—" She couldn't force the word "us" from her lips.

"No. It didn't start out that way." Carsten's eyes pleaded with her. He held out his hand. "Listen, Maddie—"

"Don't call me Maddie." Her eyes filled with tears, and she hated that more than the hurt threatening to crack her heart in half "You lied to me." She stood abruptly.

"Don't go." Carsten reached out to stop her, but pulled his hand back as she jerked out of his reach.

"Why? Because it's not *safe*?" The word shot like a dart from her tongue. "You might be paid to be around me, but that doesn't mean I can't make a decision to go upstairs on my own." She was a grown woman, and while her father never saw her that way, she thought Carsten had.

Her hands shook, and she clenched them into fists to stop the trembling. "I'm used to betrayal from my father. He was never around and never knew I existed growing up." She laughed, a short, hard laugh devoid of any humor. "I guess that's why he never realized that I have."

Carsten flinched, reaching for her again before thinking better of it and dropping his arm to his side. "I didn't want it to come to this, Madison."

"So you wish you had kept lying?" How had she possibly thought she was in love with this man? He was no better than her father was. In fact, he was worse.

Her heart throbbed a protest, but she couldn't stop long enough to address it. If she did, she'd crack into a thousand pieces.

Carsten sighed. "No, that's not it either." He paused. "Tell me something." He moved toward her, grasping her hands firmly in his. This time, he didn't let go when she tried to pull away.

"Let me go!" She struggled harder, and the fact that she couldn't wrench free just made her madder. Was she truly as weak and incapable as her father believed her to be? As Carsten now believed her to be? Tears filled her eyes.

Carsten loosened his grip, but didn't let go completely. "Just answer one question, Madison."

"What?" She quit fighting, but wouldn't meet his gaze. Her lip quivered, and she bit down on it until she tasted metal. Blood. But she wouldn't break down and cry. Not in front of him. Not until she was back in her room.

At this point, facing down an unknown intruder possibly lurking upstairs sounded like a much better alternative to Carsten's lies.

"Why was it all right for me to protect you before? Why wasn't it a problem for you to cry on my shoulder and share your fears with me?" He gently shook her hands, and she darted a glimpse into his eyes just long enough to regret it. "You already trusted me to keep you safe. What changed, Maddie? Why was it fine then, but not now?"

Easy. This time, her gaze locked into his and a strength she didn't know she had flooded her weary veins.. "Because then, I thought it came from your heart. Not from my father's checkbook."

She yanked her hands free, and felt her heart tear away from him in the same fluid motion.

18

Madison paced in her room. She needed air. She needed space. But mostly, she needed to get far away from Carsten.

She walked to the window and raised the pane, staring out into the night. A floodlight lit the backyard, and she could see the silhouettes of the horses in the paddock. One lifted its head and whinnied, a chilling sound in the darkness. The storm clouds were rolling by, bringing a brisk wind that lifted Madison's hair and offered a feeble attempt to calm the fire that still raged in her heart.

She turned her face up to the wind and closed her eyes, breathing deeply. She knew how the horse felt. She too, wanted—no, longed—for her freedom. She was so tired of being manipulated. She felt just like the animal inside the fence. "You can jump," she whispered to the stallion. "Just jump the fence, and you're home free."

Madison rested her elbows on the windowsill, realizing that she could take her own advice. Nothing was physically holding her here. She had originally thought she would be safe on the ranch, but obviously not. If someone had broken into her room, they could get to her anywhere. The thought made the hair on her arms rise. She shut the window with a bang and locked it, letting the curtains fall back into place.

A knock sounded on the closed guest room door. Her heart skipped a beat. She pressed a hand against her chest. "Sorry, I'm indecent!" It was mostly a lie, but she wasn't up to talking to anyone, not even to Rita.

Silence was her only response. She tiptoed to the door and got down on her hands and knees, peering underneath. She could just make out the black dress shoes Carsten still wore from their date.

As he walked away, she closed her eyes tightly, forcing back the image of how handsome he had looked earlier in the evening. It had all gone so terribly wrong. Why couldn't the date have ended at that perfect moment by the front door? With that perfect kiss?

Her eyes opened abruptly. Their fairy tale was over. There would be no happy ending. Only shattered hearts, broken promises, unfulfilled dreams.

The grandfather clock downstairs rang, and Madison counted the chimes. Twelve. It seemed fitting that the romance which had started at midnight would end at the same hour, over six years later.

She began to pack.

~*~

Carsten didn't sleep well. He kept picturing the look on Madison's face when she left the living room earlier that evening. He rolled onto his side and tried to get comfortable. His eyelids might as well have been pinned open.

He punched his pillow, as much to release frustration as to fluff it. Their date had gone so perfectly. He should have known something that wonderful couldn't last. His stomach twisted as he remembered the feel of Madison in his arms, the taste of her kiss…

Carsten groaned. He was torturing himself. He had to get a grip. He had told his heart all along not to get involved, to stay focused on the job.

He'd fallen for his client.

But did it count when she'd stolen his heart long before the assignment?

He thought back to the first time he saw Madison, that cold night in Germany. The night he'd relived more times than he should have. No wonder he'd botched this.

Though it'd been inevitable. It truly had been only a matter of time before Madison figured out his official role in her life—she would've overheard a phone call between him and home office, such as when he'd called to run the plate on the black SUV back in NYC. Stolen, of course, and a dead end. Or she could have seen his gun sooner—could have felt the butt of it when they'd danced in the rain and she'd wrapped her arms around his back.

His head and throbbed at the memory. He'd messed up big, but how much of a choice had he had in the first place? He'd have told her the truth immediately if he hadn't promised her father he'd keep the secret.

He drew a tight breath as that realization dawned for the first time all night. Teddy Lawrence would have to be told of this change in operation, ideally first thing in the morning before he heard from Madison.

Carsten's stomach rolled, and he groaned. He'd

dealt with wealthy, entitled clients before, but none like Teddy Lawrence. Madison's issues with her father were legit, and probably ran a lot deeper than Carsten could ever realize.

And he'd made it ten times worse. Would she ever forgive him?

Her stricken, betrayed face was the last thing he saw before he drifted off to sleep.

~*~

Madison was gone with the sunrise, the scenery flying past the window of the bus as the wheels carried her farther from the Running R. She had imagined that traveling by bus would be the safest route. Too much traceable information was available in a rental car. Besides, she had no idea where to go. Instead, she had paid cash and hoped for the best. Maybe that would be enough to keep her undetected.

At this point, she wasn't sure if she was running from Carsten, or from whoever was pursuing her. She just wanted to be safe—physically, and emotionally. At the moment, she had no control of either. Especially over her traitorous heart. If she were honest with herself, she missed him already. Or maybe just who she thought he was.

Now she knew the truth. He was a liar. A manipulator.

Yet she couldn't get him out of her mind.

What did that say about her? Too many fairytales had warped her sense of reality. She was still trying to see only the positive and not the glaring negatives right in her face.

More like happily ever never. The clock had

struck, and she hadn't left a shoe behind. It was over.

Madison rested her head against the back of the seat, eyelids drooping. She wanted to stay awake and alert, but her efforts were failing fast. She hadn't gone to bed the night before, but rather had sneaked out of the house with as many things as she could carry comfortably in a duffel bag, and walked to the bus stop a few miles down the road.

Madison shuddered, remembering the long walk in the pitch of night.

She'd convinced herself that she'd imagined the whole ordeal in her room. No one, not even a ransacker, would break into her room miles from New York just to clean out her hairbrush. That was ridiculous.

She wasn't entirely sure now whether that were true.

But one thing was certain: she couldn't stay at the ranch a minute longer. She couldn't face Carsten at the breakfast table, and try to pretend that she didn't love him, that this hadn't wrecked her. She couldn't ignore the intensity of the feelings that still lingered, despite the betrayal boiling deep. . She had to give them time to simmer away.

And the part of her heart that was still able to beat was determined to prove—both to Carsten and her dad—that she wasn't a little girl anymore. She could take care of herself. Hadn't she done so this far all along? She'd created a successful business, and lived off her own means.

She could make it back to New York alone, and forget this entire drama ever happened.

One bus had let her off at another station, and

she had purchased a ticket for as far south as she could afford with the amount of cash in her purse. She wasn't sure where she was going, or even where she was at the moment. Idaho, maybe? The passing countryside offered no explanation.

She needed a plan. She couldn't ride all the way to New York on her dwindling funds But she didn't want to use her credit cards to purchase a plane ticket. Her dad would be monitoring those—and who knew who else.

When had her life become a suspense novel?

Madison stared out the window into the hazy morning sky. Hopelessness tugged at her spirit, and she embraced the coldness that came with it. Were Carsten and Rita awake? Did they miss her? Had they noticed she was gone yet?

A twinge of guilt flickered in her stomach, but Madison ignored it. All it took was remembering what Carsten had done to her, and the guilt was replaced by burning indignation. She had kissed him, had offered a piece of her heart in exchange for his, and he'd slapped it away with the truth. Just like her father always had.

Rita, however, had been nothing but kind to her throughout her entire stay. Madison remembered the note she had scrawled and left sitting on the kitchen counter.

Rita—

Thanks for everything. I'm sorry I had to leave like this. Maybe you'll understand. I appreciate your sweet hospitality, and hopefully, we'll meet again someday.

Gratefully,
Madison

Madison wiped away a tear from each eye and continued to stare out the window. She relived each of Carsten's words, his seemingly reluctant admittance of the truth. Was it all an act? Had he meant anything? She was such a fool. With each memory, each thought, she placed a brick on the wall she was building around her heart. Hopefully, by the time she reached her destination, wherever that might be, the barrier would be firmly in place.

Then no one would be able to hurt her again.

19

The bus stopped two hours later, and Madison stepped into the station anxious to stretch her legs. Her stomach growled, and she realized she had skipped breakfast. She scrounged in the bottom of her purse and came up with enough change for some food. Purchasing a sausage biscuit from the deli next door, she sat down on a bench by the station to eat while awaiting the next bus.

Her cellphone rang. She jumped, dropping the biscuit in her lap and fumbling to retrieve the phone from her purse. Her heart pounded. *Carsten? Shan?* Had she been discovered? Or was it her father, checking in again?

Bitterness filled her mouth at the thought. She had no desire to speak with him. She was used to his antics, but secretly hiring a bodyguard to pose as a client? That was low, even for him.

A pang struck at not getting to finish the job on the beautiful ranch house. Salt in the wound.

She didn't recognize the number blinking on the caller I.D. Should she answer? Mouth dry, Madison flipped open the phone and pushed the "on" button. "Hello?" She held her breath. If it was her father, she'd just hang up.

"Maddie!"

Madison winced at the familiar, accented voice that still sent a shiver down her back. She willed steel into her spine. He deserved nothing from her.

"Carsten." She kept her voice tight. *Hang up, hang up*. But she couldn't do it.

"Where are you? We've been searching the ranch since before dawn. Are you all right?"

He sounded so sincere. But he couldn't be. He didn't care—or if he did, it was because if he lost her, he was going to get fired from his job as guardian.

No, that wasn't true. He wasn't heartless, even if he was a liar. Madison closed her eyes, wishing her wall were more secure. Guilt was seeping through the cracks, trailed by something dangerously close to regret. "I had to leave, Carsten. I left Rita a note."

"She found it. But we didn't think you would have gotten far. Where are you?" Carsten asked a second time, his voice firmer now. She supposed not many people told him no.

But she'd lived that life long enough under her dad.

She sighed. "I'm fine, Carsten. I'm safe I'm heading south currently. That's all you need to know." The last thing she needed was for him to come after her. One more look into those blue eyes and she'd be toast.

Her wall needed time to cement.

Silence filled the line.

"Madison, I know you're upset about all of this, but I want you to come home. Right now."

He sounded strangely like her father. Commands, always commands. She swiped crumbs off her lap onto the concrete ground, not bothering to lower her voice even as several people walked past to catch their bus. "And where exactly is home?

With my father, who pretends I don't exist? Or perhaps it's with you, the man I trusted who has been lying to me about everything since the day we met? No wait, I know. It's in New York, where a crazy person is following me!" She swiped back an angry tear. Her emotions were on full boil, and she feared she'd erupt at any moment.

"I'm not sure where you belong, Madison." He sounded tired now, as though he'd aged in the hours she'd been gone. "I don't know where your home is."

He paused a beat. "But I want you to know that my home is anywhere you are."

No. He wasn't supposed to be nice. That made it worse.

He was supposed to yell back at her. Make her angry. Then she could leave and not look back.

Why did he sound so sincere when his feelings obviously weren't? Her resolve came back in full force. Nothing about their relationship—could they even call it that?—had been normal. She couldn't trust any of it.

"I'm sorry." She ducked her head, her voice low. "I can't trust you. You lied to me, and ganged up on me with my father. I don't feel safe anymore—with you or with anyone."

She had to end this and move on. From here on out, it was just her. And her business. She could focus on that instead of her broken heart. Her friendship with Shan. Her next career goal. There was plenty to keep her occupied until Carsten faded from her heart.

The fact that he hadn't in six years was slightly discouraging.

"I hope you'll change your mind." Carsten's voice softened, and held a hope that tore at Madison's heart.

She squeezed her eyes shut. She couldn't do this. She had to get off the phone. She opened her mouth, but Carsten changed the subject.

"I found out who broke into your room."

Madison opened her eyes and sat up straighter on the bench. "What? Who?" Had it been that simple? Was the nightmare over?

"It was Mitch."

What? Mitch was her stalker? "I don't understand. Why would he do that?" It didn't make any sense at all. Had Mitch been in New York? She had a dozen questions but couldn't get any of them out.

"I questioned the staff this morning, asked if anyone had seen or heard anything suspicious last night. The more I revealed, the more Mitch squirmed. I took him aside and he confessed to it." Carsten sounded tired. "But only to that."

Madison's mind reeled. "So then Mitch isn't the person who was chasing me in New York?" Her heart sank. It wasn't over. Mitch was a separate problem, not the main one.

"Unfortunately, no. Mitch said that he was jealous over your rejection of him and dating me, and he wanted to get to you. He had no idea that you were at the ranch under protective custody. He felt badly about scaring you when he realized the truth."

Wow. She'd never have thought. Mitch had been leering and creepy, but that was an entirely different level of vengeful. Who *did* that? She shivered, grateful she was away from his piercing stare.

"He's fired, of course, with the understanding that if he steps back onto the ranch, I'll shoot first and ask questions later. He left somewhat peaceably."

Madison shook her head. "At least that mystery is solved." But the larger one remained. So she had been safe on the ranch after all.

What about now?

She cast an uneasy look over her shoulder. She had fled safety, assuming it was dangerous, yet had possibly run straight into it. Was her stalker still in New York, or had he been on his way to Montana?

What if they met in the middle?

She shook off the unease. That was the exact attitude which had made her weak and incapable. She was strong. She could handle herself.

Carsten rambled on. "This means that whoever was bothering you in New York is most likely still in New York. Right now, we have no reason to believe that they caught up to you in Montana."

"Drop the phone."

Madison froze as cool metal pressed into her back. A million thoughts ran through her mind in an incoherent jumble, ending in one thought.

She was foolish.

She slowly lowered the phone the bench beside her, careful to keep it turned on as she did. Would Carsten hear any of this? Would he know what to do? Her heart pounded as she debated whether to look over her shoulder.

"Move forward now, and don't even think about causing a scene."

Madison's mind raced with possibilities as she stood on wobbly legs She had the clarity of mind to grab her purse as she made her way from the bench. *Where does this guy want me to go?* She walked rigidly in front of him, desperate to see his face. Would she recognize him?

Carsten's voice, panicked and tiny from her phone now several feet behind them, filled the air around them. The man cursed and slapped the phone off the bench and onto the ground, stomping it with a booted foot. It was all she saw before the gun jammed back into her spine and her kidnapper instructed her to walk slow.

She didn't want to upset him, but she also didn't want to move too far from the public area. Maybe someone would notice her distress and help. She rubbed her damp palms down the front of her jeans and took a few more tentative steps.

Her captor had the gun pressed firmly against her ribcage, and he was walking closely beside her. To anyone in the crowd, they would look like couple just taking a stroll. She darted a sideways glance, hoping to catch a glimpse of his face. But he had a baseball cap pulled down low, and wore casual clothes. He looked just like any other person in the crowd. No recognizable features, nothing that stood out or screamed danger to anyone in passing. How was she going to get free? Was he going to kill her?

Madison gulped, fighting back fear. This was not the time to panic. She had to think clearly and find a way out of this mess. *God, a little help this time!*

Once away from the crowd at the bus station, the man grabbed her arm, and spun her to face him. She averted her gaze, afraid to look at him now that she could. "I don't want to have to use this thing, but I will. We can make this easy or hard."

She vaguely recognized the voice, but had no idea how or from where. Daring to look into his face, she noticed the whites of his eyes. Her adrenaline surged. This guy was either insane or plain nervous. He didn't exactly seem like a real criminal.

But that gun sure looked real enough.

20

Madison winced against the shove that propelled her toward a car parked at a meter. She mentally noted the make and model just before a blindfold was slipped over her eyes and she was shoved into the backseat.

"I'm sorry."

Surprised, she jerked her head to the side as the door slammed closed after her. What kind of kidnapper apologized before pushing their captive into a getaway car? This man really must be crazy. Or maybe she was hearing things through the adrenaline that refused to stop coursing through her body.

What if he really was that insane? She shivered, fighting for a measure of control. Just as quickly, she remembered that Someone else already had it. God was still God. She needed to wait and do her part when the time came... assuming God gave her that opportunity. Was He watching? She could really use a reassuring sign right now.

Madison braced against the seat, heart pounding, as she another door clicked open and closed. An engine roared to life. "Lay down." The voice snapped, but the tone held more nervous energy than agitation.

She obeyed, draping blindly over the seats, and licked her dry lips. Leather pressed into her cheek. A hymn suddenly blared from the radio, and for one delirious moment, Madison felt the urge to giggle. Was that her sign?

The radio shut off abruptly, and the gun's safety clicked. She sobered fast.

"Don't try anything stupid back there."

Yes. She definitely knew that voice. Maybe if she could place it, she'd have a lead, or know how to work the situation to her advantage. The doors locked and the car peeled out, tires squealing.

Madison began to pray.

~*~

Carsten slammed his fist into the wall. The sheetrock crumbled, leaving a hole the size of his hand. He barely noticed the pain. He called the police and reported the emergency and then paced anxiously as he dialed his partner for back up. He needed to know who was the owner of that SUV from New York.

The phone rang, three times. Four. With each ringing repetition, the same fact cycled through his head.

He had failed. The events that had led him back into Madison's life had at one point seemed orchestrated by God. But now she was in danger. Had he misinterpreted God's agenda?

He needed a plan—whether the Lord was willing to help him or not.

Or his partner, for that matter, who wasn't answering the phone. He snapped the phone shut, wishing he could throw it across the room too, but he'd need it later.

He had to think.

"Is everything OK?" Rita bustled into the living room, coming to an abrupt stop as she saw the damage to the wall. "Carsten. What happened?"

"They have her." He still couldn't believe she'd been snatched while he'd been right there on the other end of the line. And all she'd told him was that she'd been heading south. Darn her pride!

Rita's eyes opened wide. "Who has who?"

"They have Madison. I don't know who, or where she is. When I called her, she was on her cellphone heading south." He ran his hands over his jaw, his two day stubble bristling under his fingers. "I told her about Mitch, hoping that'd convince her to come back here. The next thing I know, a deep voice commands her to drop the phone and then we lost our connection."

Rita pressed a hand to her heart. "Should we call the police? Put out a search bulletin?"

"Already done. Now I've got to head the same direction and pray I can get a lead on the way." Carsten withdrew his hands from his face, realizing for the first time the blood on his knuckles. Then he took in the damage to the wall and groaned. "Sorry, Rita. I'll fix that."

"It's all right, my boy." Rita handed Carsten the rag she had been holding so he could wipe his hands. "I know that you'll have Madison back here to finish fixing up and decorating this place in no time." Her steady tone proved she actually meant it. He wished he could be as certain.

Carsten wiped his hands and tucked the rag in his pocket. "I'm glad you have faith in me." "I'm going to look around Madison's room before I leave. Maybe she left a clue as to where she was going.

Grab that note for me that she left you." He doubted it would reveal anything he hadn't already considered a dozen times, but just in case. Besides, Rita looked as if she could use an assignment.

He took the stairs two at a time. Stepping into Madison's guest room, he took a deep breath, filling his senses with her remaining presence. The room still carried the distinct smell of her perfume.

Carsten released the air in his lungs and began a thorough search. He pulled open every drawer and even looked under the bed. Though she had left a lot behind, he found nothing to go by. Lord? Anything?

Conviction pricked at his urge to pray only when he was truly desperate. Would God even hear him?

The angel Shan had sent from the office toppled to the floor as he set the mattress back down onto the frame. *Thunk.*

Carsten frowned and walked around the side of the bed to pick it up. Why would a stuffed doll make such a loud noise?

He picked up the doll then perched himself on the edge of the mattress, turning the angel over and over in his hands. It felt heavier than he would have imagined. Carsten was no fool, he'd seen enough in his career to know that when his instinct told him something was amiss, something was amiss. But what?

He reached into his jeans for a pocketknife. He flipped open the blade and cut into the fabric of the doll's dress, praying Madison would forgive him for destroying her stuffed angel if his guess wasn't correct.

He wasn't disappointed.

Carsten pulled out some of the cotton stuffing and stared. The diamond was the size of a walnut. The sun streaming through the window reflected off its surface and sent patterns of light dancing across the ceiling.

"I think I just realized why your apartment was ransacked, Madison." He spoke the words with a mixture of awe and dismay. It was easy to see why someone would want the jewel back at any cost. The thing had to be worth a fortune.

How in the world had she come into possession of it?

Adrenaline along with a surge of unfiltered fear for Madison's safety urged him into action. He mumbled a quick prayer of thanks as he stuffed the diamond back into the angel. He'd deal with his prayer life later.

He hurried down the stairs. "Rita! We've got trouble."

He had answers now—one of which he didn't like at all. The motivation behind the kidnapping put Madison into greater danger than he'd initially feared.

Maybe he'd figure out his prayer life

~*~

They drove for what felt like an eternity. Time passed in increments too slow to measure. Finally, the car pulled to a stop, and Madison heard the drivers' side door open once again.

She accidentally hit her head as she got out of the car, still blindfolded. "Ow!" Her sharp cry of distress came out unintentionally. She didn't want to look weak to her captor. She reached up to rub the offended spot.

"Ssh!" A voice hissed in her ear. She cringed and bit her lip, determined to keep silent as she was ushered forward. Another door opened, and she stepped from the sunlight into darkness. Cold seeped over her skin. They were inside a building. A cold, damp building.

She stumbled over something and the grip on her arm tightened. "There's a staircase," the voice offered gruffly.

Madison groped her way down the steps, wishing with all her heart she could see where she was going. She had tried to keep mental notes about what she had felt and heard since her abductor had blindfolded her, but it was all a blur now. She couldn't get back to the bus station if her life depended on it.

And it might.

Scraping echoed from across the room. Madison lifted her head in surprise. What was that? Someone else was here? She didn't know if that brought her relief or more fear.

A voice, different than the first one, began speaking softly, but in a harsh and condescending tone. She couldn't make out the words and didn't know whether they were directed at her.

Madison shifted her weight, her pulse racing. The grip on her arm eased a bit, but she refused to relax. Her muscles were wound tighter than coiled springs. She had to stay ready, alert...prepared.

But for what? Various scenarios flashed through her mind, each worse than the one before. She shivered.

"Remove the blindfold," the deep voice ordered

loudly. "Tie her hands."

Madison held her breath, and suddenly she could see. She was standing in a dark, sparsely furnished room, with only two chairs and a small desk occupying the far side. It looked to be a basement. Her shoulders slumped as she realized the lack of windows.

She noticed that the two men in front of her looked similar. Brothers? Cousins? Madison hoped she wasn't going to be sticking around long enough to find out those kinds of details.

She clenched her teeth as the thin one tied her hands behind her back with the blindfold.

Wait a minute. She could see them. Her heart sank. How could the men let her live if she could identify them?

Fresh fear coursed through her veins in a dark wave, and a sour taste filled her mouth. She had to do something.

"Why am I here?" She lifted her chin and tried to look confidant, despite the fact that her hands were shaking in their bindings.

The bigger man laughed, an evil sound, one she never wanted to hear again. It would haunt her dreams for months—assuming she lived that long. "You really don't know, do you?"

The man closest to her chuckled, too, though it sounded more forced. Was he not a ready volunteer to this kidnapping? He seemed to be going through the motions, not enjoying the scene before him like the bigger one.

"You have something that we need back." The bigger man walked closer to Madison with exaggerated patience, speaking slowly and deliberately as if she were stupid. He finished his sentence so close to her face she could feel his breath on her cheeks. She flinched as the strong smell of cigar smoke penetrated the air. If they had removed her blindfold in order to increase the intimidation factor, it was unfortunately working.

"And we're not patient men. I hope your family is feeling...cooperative." A slow grin spread across his broad jaw.

They were holding her for ransom?

She tasted the resentment that bubbled from the depths of her past. It was just one more reason to despise being Teddy Lawrence's daughter. What had he gotten her into?

The urge to throw a major pity party swept her up and almost consumed. Why couldn't she have had a normal father? One that took her to get ice cream and taught her how to ride a bike and panicked when she got her driver's license? Not one that hired guardians behind her back, lied regularly, and got her kidnapped?

"Have a seat, sweetheart. We have a few calls to make to Daddy." The man picked up his phone and waved it at her.

She remained standing in defiance. "I'm fine standing."

The older man shot the younger one a look, and then with three long strides he was once again standing directly in front of her. He raised his hand and threatened to slap her. Madison instinctively ducked, heart in her throat.

"The next one won't be a warning. Sit down!" A vein popped out on his forehead. He wasn't kidding.

Fear clenching her heart in a vise, Madison slid down against the wall to a sitting position. *Don't you dare cry!*

She focused on the smaller man as the second one began dialing across the basement. This guy, her actual kidnapper, seemed much less intense. Maybe she could gain his sympathy.

The more she studied him, the more it seemed that he was an unwillingly participant in this charade. His jerky movements and constant eye darting proved as much.

"Hey." Madison whispered to him, after a quick glance at the older man on the phone. "I didn't mean to make him mad."

The younger guy looked across the room with a nervous expression. He shoved his hands in his pockets. "Oh, he's not mad. Not yet, anyway."

Great.

Madison subtly studied the man in front of her. He seemed to be suffering from a permanent caffeine overdose—

constantly moving, rocking on his heels, shuffling his feet. He looked like a person consumed by guilt, or perhaps shame. She felt a twinge of sorrow for the guy. It evaporated quickly as she remembered the feel of the gun pressed against her ribcage.

She cleared her throat. "Are you brothers?" She dared to ask. That would explain a lot. The look on his face answered her question, though his lips said nothing. He turned away.

Madison racked her brain, hoping to get some kind of leverage out of the information she had gathered. Her mind was a blank. How could she use the knowledge to free herself? Could she turn one brother against the other?

Feeling completely helpless, she rested her head against the wall behind her. It was in God's hands. At the moment, there was nothing she could do to help herself.

So she prayed

And kicked herself for her pride having gotten her into this mess.

21

Carsten grabbed for the ringing phone in the passenger seat beside him Was it Madison? *"Hallo?"* His heart hammered in his chest. She had to be OK, had to be safe…

"I would fire you, but I need you to get my daughter back."

Carsten bit his tongue in an effort to check his words at Teddy Lawrence's comment. He was stressed and emotionally wired, and the last thing he wanted to do was exchange insults with Madison's father. Getting her back, that needed to be his only concern.

He released a quick breath. "What do you know?"

"I know I just received a call from someone demanding a hefty ransom. What I don't know is why you had yet to inform me that Madison is missing!" Carsten could hear the strain in Teddy's voice.

"Is that all they want?" Carsten held his breath, purposely ignoring Teddy's other question. Maybe the diamond wasn't involved. Maybe they just wanted some cash and this whole ordeal could be settled.

"They also mentioned something about a diamond Madison had taken from them. I assume you know more about that than I do, too." Sarcasm dripped from the older man's voice.

Carsten's heart sunk. He knew it couldn't have been that easy. "I found it a little while ago." He paused, bracing for the worst. "What were the instructions?"

"One million dollars in cash by midnight tomorrow." Teddy's tone was stressed. "They're going to call back with the location."

Carsten gathered his resolve. He was a professional. He would treat this like any other case. The fact that he loved the woman involved was irrelevant. The goal was to get her home safely. Anything past that was just a bonus.

Not that Madison would give him the time of day after what he'd done to her. She might need rescuing from the kidnappers, but he doubted she needed a knight in shining armor to save her heart. That wall was proving impenetrable.

"You screwed up, Carsten." Teddy's harsh words brought him back to the present.

He counted to three before responding with a clenched fist at his side. "Sir, with all due respect, she left the ranch on her own."

"Under your watch."

Carsten pressed his lips together to hold back another sharp retort. He couldn't argue. Madison was in danger, and it was his fault. In trying to give Madison her space after their big fight, he'd not watched her closely enough. He could accept that it was his responsibility.

But he wouldn't accept it was the end of the story.

He could fix this. He had to. Determination tinged with desperation filled his senses. This didn't have to end the same way. It might be too late for his dad, but it wasn't too late for Madison.

"We'll get her back."

"I have no doubt of that." Now Lawrence sounded steely—more like the powerful, wealthy man he was. "I hope you realize this changes our financial agreement."

Carsten shut his eyes in an effort to control his rage. He couldn't believe what Lawrence had just said. Was he more concerned about money than about his daughter's welfare? What kind of father was he? The last thing on Carsten's mind was the fee Teddy Lawrence promised him in exchange for keeping Madison in the dark about their arrangement. Carsten only wanted Maddie safe. He wanted to see her smile again, hear her laughter tease the air between them, feel her lips against his...

"I'm aware of that, and I couldn't care less about the money. My concern is getting Madison safely home."

"Then you'll have no problem getting the money together for the ransom."

Carsten's jaw dropped. "Sir?" His heartbeat hammered out a frantic rhythm. Surely, he had misunderstood.

"Madison was *your* responsibility. You let her down. I expect you to have the million dollars as requested."

The man must be joking. Carsten closed his eyes. "I don't have that kind of cash, Mr. Lawrence." Not even close. What game was this man playing?

"I've paid you for your services to this point. Use that for starters, and I suggest you find the rest as soon as possible. I'll call you when I hear back about the location."

Carsten looked at the phone in surprise as the click sounded on the other line, disconnecting the call. How could a father be that heartless? His daughter was being held for ransom, and he refused to pay?

Shock waves reverberated through Carsten's mind. Maybe Madison was right about her father after all. Who could do such a thing? What would happen if Carsten couldn't come up with the cash? Would Teddy pay then?

He couldn't assume.

Carsten sat for a moment, staring at the phone in his hand, mentally reviewing his bank account. Then he released a heavy sigh and stood up. He knew what he had to do.

~*~

Madison shifted positions in the uncomfortable chair, her hands still tied behind her back. Joseph and Lance, as she had come to discover their names during one of their frequent arguments, had allowed her to move into the chair when she started complaining about the cold floor. She'd been sincere, though had been partly curious how far she could push them and exactly how heartless they were. She needed to learn her boundaries with those two, quick.

Joseph and Lance now talked in hushed tones from across the room. But not hushed enough. She stared at the ceiling, pretending not to listen, and cast occasional sidelong glances their direction.

"I don't think that's a good idea. It's too much

money." Lance shook his head, and then immediately backed down when Joseph muttered a response too softly for Madison to catch.

"The girl's not even his own daughter. What if he doesn't pay?" Lance questioned loudly.

Madison's eyes widened. She wasn't *what*?

Joseph shushed his brother, and glanced in Madison's direction. She quickly arranged her features to show complete nonchalance, though her heart threatened to burst out of her chest. The room spun, and she closed her eyes briefly. The talking resumed, this time too quietly for her to hear.

Madison's mind raced. What were they talking about? He had just spoken to her dad on the phone. What did he mean, not her real father?

She struggled to believe they were mistaken, but what if they weren't? She forced the thought to the back of her mind. Whether the statement was true didn't matter at the moment. She needed to focus on her current predicament. Like getting out of there. She cast a look around the room again, but came up with no new ideas. There were no windows, and the only door was inches away from the two brothers. She searched for anything she could use as a weapon, but saw nothing that would give her any power over the two men.

Madison rubbed her bound wrists against her pants, wishing the rope didn't itch so badly. It was already leaving a splotchy red rash on her hands. She fought the urge to cough. Would they give her a drink if she asked? It had also been hours since she ate half of the biscuit from the bus station. She chose to ignore her empty stomach for now, but decided she needed water or she would dehydrate on the spot.

"Excuse me." She cleared her throat, and the two men across the room stopped talking abruptly and looked in her direction.

Joseph raised his eyebrows.

Was that permission to speak? She swallowed hard. "I was wondering if I could have a glass of water."

Joseph studied her with a dark gaze, and after a moment, nodded to his brother. "In the desk drawer."

Lance retrieved a bottle of water from the desk and handed it to Madison. He looked as if he wanted to say something, but held back. Instead, he removed the cap and held it to Madison's lips. The water was lukewarm.

She drank deeply, not caring that it dribbled down her chin and splashed onto her shirt. When she was finished, she nodded at Lance, and thanked him as he set the bottle beside her.

"Will there be anything else, my lady?" Joseph's sarcasm was thick. He ambled over to where she sat in the chair, and leaned down in her face. "Any other needs in which we can attend?"

The gleam in his eye suggested something vulgar, and Madison inwardly cringed. Outwardly, she set her chin. "Absolutely not." She forced herself to stare unshaken back into his eyes. But the evil she saw beneath the surface startled her, and she dropped her gaze.

"I might be inclined to argue with you." Joseph cupped her face in his hand and raised her chin. She jerked away, cheeks burning from his contact, adrenaline flooding as she prepared to fight.

"Joseph." Lance spoke up suddenly from across the room, tapping his watch. "What about that errand we need to run? To set up the swap? Remember?"

Joseph groaned. "Go do it yourself. I can stay here with her. We can get to know each other." He reached for Madison's face again. She ducked in protest, holding her breath. Lance tapped his shoe in a rhythm against the basement floor. "I can't. They know my face, remember?"

Joseph threw his arms in the air in frustration. "All right! Let's go."

He grabbed a few things that Madison couldn't identify out of the top drawer of the desk and then slammed it closed. He locked it with a key that he slipped into his shirt pocket and stalked out of the room, mumbling the entire time.

Lance, gaze averted, started for the door as well.

"Hey." Madison tilted her head.

Lance turned.

"Thanks." She knew he had purposely distracted his brother, and she was more grateful than she could ever express.

Lance met her gaze for a moment and then nodded. He stepped outside the room, and she heard a key turn in the lock.

Madison shifted in the chair, trying to find a more comfortable position. She wished she had a blanket. A roach darted across the room. She shivered, and drew her legs underneath her in the chair. It appeared as though she were here for the night.

22

"They want to make the swap at midnight in an abandoned warehouse in Martinsdale. We're supposed to bring both the cash and the diamond."

Carsten ran his hand over the leather bag sitting in front of him as he listened to Teddy's instructions over the phone. He never would have thought that much money could fit inside such a small bag, but it did.

"I'll be there. Where should I meet you?" He unzipped the bag to check on the money for the fifth time. It was enough to make a man nauseous. Ransom money. Dirty, though the bills sparkled new in their packaging. He quickly averted his gaze and zipped the bag closed again. He set it on the floor at his feet.

"What do you mean, meet me? This is your show." Teddy sounded surprised.

Carsten jerked his head up. "What? You want me to go alone?"

"Isn't that what you do?" Teddy asked with disdain.

"I have before, of course, but, sir, she's your daughter..."

"I know she's my daughter!" Teddy's voice cracked with emotion, and Carsten backed off.

"Fine. I'll do it by myself." He listened to the rest of the instructions and then hung up the phone.

Carsten pushed his hair back in a rough motion, then looked at his watch. Only 8:30 p.m. This was going to be a long night.

But then again, the day had already felt like it would never end. He hadn't slept since he realized Madison had left. How could he rest not knowing where she was, or if she was all right? What if the kidnappers were lying about her condition?

Carsten once again felt the urge to pray. He would never be able to pull off this case without God's help. He was too emotionally involved to be as objective as necessity demanded. That was the first rule in his field—not to get attached. People got hurt when hearts were involved.

But it was much too late for that.

"I know You're there." Carsten whispered as he dropped his head to rest against the tabletop. "I still don't understand why You do what You do, or why You sometimes allow what You allow. But I need help, God."

Tempted to bargain, but knowing that wasn't how God worked, he released a sigh and struggled to surrender instead.

He continued to pray as the minutes ticked by, bringing his heart closer to God, and bringing time closer to the inevitable midnight hour.

~*~

Madison woke suddenly as she heard a shuffling at the door. What time was it? She had no idea how long she'd been in the basement. She shifted in her uncomfortable position in the chair and tried to calm her heartbeat.

The door swung open, and Joseph and Lance

stood framed in the doorway.

Madison felt the last remaining bits of hope drift away as she watched the men go to the desk and start laying out paperwork. She should have known better than to think Carsten would have already found her. It had only been a day or two, and because of her stubborn pride, he didn't even know where to begin to look.

She berated herself again as she remembered the opportunity that had been given to her during their phone call at the bus station. God had given her a way out, and she had stubbornly turned her nose up at the offer. Would she get another chance? Madison blinked back a rush of tears. What if she never saw him again?

Maybe it was the damp basement. Maybe it was just common sense settling in. But somehow, gratitude for all she'd been given began to sink in. She had been offered the chance to love Carsten, and she had thrown it away because of her own personal issues with trust. Now she might never get the opportunity again.

Suddenly it didn't matter that he'd lied to her. He had done so in order to protect her, keep her safe. That was a *good* thing. Carsten loved her, and as much as she hated to admit it, she loved him back.

Frustration balled in her throat. Would she ever get to tell him? To ask forgiveness for the way she behaved?

Joseph took a knife that had at least a four-inch blade out of the desk, and Madison's heart stopped, then pounded hard and fast in her chest. She cringed as he drew closer, and then she realized with a start that he was just going to cut the rope off her hands.

"You have to eat something." Joseph sliced through her binds with one quick motion.

Madison drew her hands up to her chest and rubbed at the raw places on her wrists. They were red and sore. She hoped the rope burns wouldn't leave scars. She didn't need any more reminders of this horrible place.

Then again, she was still assuming she would get out eventually. If her father brought the money, would they really let her go? It would be stupid if they did. She could pick them out of a lineup. Were they too dumb to realize that?

Well, she wasn't going to remind them.

She turned as Joseph pulled some packages of peanut butter crackers from his shirt pocket. "Here." He thrust them at her. "Bring the water!"

Lance handed Madison a bottle of water and she felt like crying with relief. She mumbled a quick thank you before tearing into the food.

The men watched her silently for a moment, and then turned back to their own business. Food had never tasted so good. The crackers crumbled easily, and she knew she must look ridiculous, shoving the food into her mouth as if it were her last meal. The thought made her stomach clench, and for a moment, she thought she would throw up. What if these crackers were her last meal?

A lifetime of regrets attacked her mind. They flashed through her memory frame by frame, much like the scenes outside the windows on the bus had done on ride over.

She as a little girl, holding up a coloring book to her father and begging him to play with her, only to have him claim he was too busy. Dressing herself for the first time as a child and seeking her mother's compliments, but instead, hearing her laugh with disdain and order the maid to change her clothes. Riding by herself to church services in a limousine because her parents had more pressing matters in which to attend.

Then herself at age eighteen, walking behind her mother and father through the streets of Germany, wishing they would just turn around and see her, truly see her, for the first time.

Madison sucked water from the bottle, wishing it would rinse the memories from her soul. If she were to die today, what would she have accomplished? Would her only legacy be the designs she had left in people's homes? She wanted so much more than that.

She put the bottle in her lap and bit into the last cracker. She wanted a husband to love. She wanted children. She wanted to start a new heritage that her kids could be proud of; not cringe over as she did her own childhood.

"It's time." Joseph announced, breaking into Madison's heavy thoughts. He stood abruptly, and her stomach lurched. She couldn't tell if it was from nerves or from eating so fast.

Madison finished the last of the water and dropped the bottle to the ground. Lance bound her hands once again. She flinched as the rope brushed the sensitive spots on her skin. Lance looked down at her red hands and cast a nervous glance over his shoulder. Joseph was digging through the desk with his back turned.

Lance reached into his pocket for a bandana, and with a quick, silent motion, tore it in half. He tied the cloth around each wrist and then secured the rope over the material.

Madison met his gaze in surprise. "Thanks." She whispered.

He nodded curtly, but didn't speak.

With that action, Madison became positive that Lance was an unwillingly participant in this chain of events. She stored that information for future use. He seemed almost as terrified of his brother as Madison was. That could help—or maybe make things worse. She wasn't sure which yet.

"Let's go!" Joseph indicated for Lance to blindfold Madison once again. She gritted her teeth as he tied a new cloth around her eyes. Madison stumbled as she was pushed ahead in their rush to get out the door. She would have hit the ground, but someone steadied her. "Careful," Lance said.

She hated this blindfold. It made the simplest things like walking difficult. She slowed her pace, ignoring Joseph's grumblings. She refused to fall or look weak in front of the men.

"She can't go as fast, Joseph. You insisted on both blindfolding her and binding her hands." Lance protested.

Joseph's heavy footsteps ahead came to a sudden stop. She followed suit. Lance ran into the back of her.

"You're both idiots." His deep voice growled. "If I didn't need this money I'd do you both in."

Madison held her breath, fearing the worst. Was he serious? What would he do after he got her father's money? Lance mumbled something unintelligible. Then he nudged her gently, and she started walking again.

The car ride this time went by quickly. Too quickly. Madison appreciated each breath of air, each moment spent alive. Before, she was certain no harm would come to her; that the men just wanted their money and things would eventually work out fine. But if Joseph was truly willing to kill his brother, then her fate didn't seem quite as promising.

The sounds of cars passing their vehicle on each side sounded louder than usual. Even her heartbeat sounded as loud as a drum. Her head was pounding, and she wanted coffee in the worst way. She fought back the insane urge to laugh. That seemed like something Shan would appreciate—wanting coffee when her life was possibly ending in the next hour.

Would she get a chance to share the story with her friend?

Minutes later, the car came to stop. Madison sat up straighter and strained to see through the material covering her eyes, but to no avail.

"He's not here yet." Lance's voice sounded nervous.

"He'll be here." Joseph's tone held a threat beneath the surface. She heard what he didn't say. *He better be.*

Madison sat quietly, wondering how her father would react to the circumstances, wondering whether these criminals would be captured and sent to prison, wondering where Carsten was... She needed to focus! She was with hardened criminals in the backseat of some car that was probably parked in the middle of nowhere, and she was thinking about the guy who broke her heart!

"There he is."

Madison's palms went damp. This was it. Whatever the future held was now only moments away. *God, help me.*

"He's getting out. Where is he going?"

"I told him to meet us inside. Come on."

The car doors opened on each side, causing the chime to sound. The dome lights flicked on. Joseph cursed. "Turn that off! How obvious can you be?"

Madison heard the sound of Lance fumbling for the controls. The light switched off. The chiming stopped. Her door opened suddenly, and she half fell, and was half pulled, from the car.

She was led blindly through the dark, her steps hesitant. She tugged discreetly at the rope binding her wrists behind her back, grateful that at least this time it wasn't cutting into her skin. She fumbled with the rope, but realized the knots were too thick to pick at with her fingernails. She held in a frustrated sigh. They stopped walking, and Madison suddenly felt another presence.

"I have the money." The voice carried a German accent. It was slight, but distinctive.

Ignoring the possible consequences, Madison shrugged the blindfold down on her face using her shoulder. It was dark, but the silhouette was unmistakable.

Carsten.

Not her father.

23

Madison went numb, first with relief then with shock as the realization of Carsten's presence sunk in. Her legs trembled, and she couldn't keep her balance. Her head began to swim. Where was her father? Had something happened to him? Or had he just not shown up?

She felt sick with betrayal. There was no way Carsten would have known where to come without her dad's involvement. He'd been told to come.

Her father had sent the hired help.

The men had yet to notice her blindfold was down, and in the darkness, she swiped at it again with her shoulder. She got the blindfold away from her mouth just in time to vomit on the grass. She fell to her knees.

"Whoa!" She heard Lance jump away in surprise, but didn't care. Nothing really mattered anymore.

She shivered as she remembered the words Lance had spoken earlier. *The girl's not even his real daughter.* It was true.

Rough hands hauled her to her feet, and she stood weakly, not caring if she fell again. Her gaze rested on the moon, hanging heavily in the sky, bathing the scene in an eerie light. It looked as far away as God felt.

"What's going on?" Carsten called out from his

position several yards away. His voice sounded odd, deeper than usual, almost as if he were trying to hide his accent.

"Nothing. Leave the money."

Joseph's demand was met by a brief silence. Then they all heard the click of a gun being taken off safety.

"Madison goes inside the warehouse, alone. Then you get your money." Carsten's voice left no room for alternate suggestions.

Someone shoved Madison. The blindfold was ripped from her head. She flinched at the rough gesture that ripped at her hair. "Go."

With her eyes only slightly adjusted to the darkness, her gaze darted left and right. An old building stood several yards to the left. She hurried toward it, opting to lean against the shack rather than go inside. She pressed her back against the cool metal and waited.

A soft thud sounded in the shadows. "There's your money."

Joseph didn't move. "What about the angel? Is the diamond in there, too?"

Madison frowned. What angel? A sudden image of the stuffed angel she had purchased online just a few months ago filled her mind's eye, and she gasped.

Then she remembered the phone call in her office several weeks ago. Lance's voice. That was it! Her stomach roiled again, and her legs began to buckle. This had all been preventable…if it hadn't been for her obsession with angels. Her obsession with Carsten…

"It's all there." Carsten's voice was tense.

Joseph nudged Lance with one hand while keeping a gun trained on Carsten with the other. Lance edged toward the bag.

"That's not Teddy." Lance announced in surprise. He stepped back.

"What? Who are you?" Joseph's voice sounded as surprised as it did angry.

"None of your concern. What is your concern is guaranteeing me that Madison is unharmed." Carsten kept his own gun aimed at Joseph.

Madison closed her eyes, wondering where her father was, wondering how all of this was going to turn out. Her eyes opened abruptly. What would she do if they killed Carsten and left her there in the dark?

"Grab the bag, you idiot!" Joseph's anger rang full force toward his brother. "As for you, your girlfriend is just fine. Very good, actually."

His suggestive tone made Madison flinch.

Carsten let out a roar and charged at Joseph. Joseph stumbled. Lance steadied his brother and shoved the bag of money into his hands. "Let's get out of here!"

Carsten dove, tackling Joseph. The bag and gun fell to the ground, and Lance scooped up the money. Carsten dodged one blow, but the second landed. He groaned and rolled to the side.

Madison ran toward the gun, heart pounding. Lance moved toward it too, but he was holding the bag of money. Madison was faster. She kicked the weapon aside and looked up just as Carsten came back at Joseph, landing a fist squarely in his face.

With a shriek, Madison jumped out of the way. Blood spewed.

Madison stood to the side, gasping for breath. Was Carsten hurt? Who was bleeding? She couldn't tell in the darkness. She saw Carsten get in a few good jabs on Joseph before Lance dropped the bag of money and hauled Carsten off his brother.

Joseph came to his feet, doubled over. He spit blood onto the ground. Then, he grabbed Madison and produced a knife from his pocket. He held it to her throat.

Madison froze, one hand gripping the arm that Joseph had wrapped around her neck. She couldn't see, couldn't think.

Couldn't pray.

"Now what, pretty boy?" Joseph's voice dripped with poison. Madison closed her eyes, barely daring to breathe. The blade pressed against her neck. She didn't swallow for fear the movement would send the knife slicing through her skin.

Carsten raised his hands in surrender. "Don't do anything stupid!"

"If you don't back up, you'll force me to just do that." Joseph's grip tightened on Madison, and she whimpered.

Carsten moved away slowly, keeping his gaze trained on Joseph. Madison gripped Joseph's arm tighter, desperately trying to loosen his grip. It wouldn't budge, and the knife pressed in closer. She stopped struggling, sensing it only made the situation worse.

Lance picked up the bag of money again. Joseph dragged Madison backwards several feet toward the car parked at the edge of the woods. She closed her eyes. She didn't want to look, didn't want to know. Was this the end? Was this their plan all along? To get the money and kill her? *God, I'm sorry I didn't do more with my life...*

Taking a step forward, hands still raised, Carsten shouted. "Let her go. You have your money!"

Madison opened her eyes, hope flooding her veins. Carsten was still there. He wouldn't let them kill her. He obviously cared more than her father did. The betrayal coursed through veins, bringing fresh pain.

She channeled the anger and reacted, bringing her elbow sharply into Joseph's stomach. At the same time, she stomped down hard on his foot. His grip loosened, and she hit him again. Joseph cursed, and in one sudden motion, shoved Madison forward, propelling her straight into Carsten's arms. They both fell hard onto the ground.

The car started. Madison struggled to sit up.

Carsten reached for a gun tucked into the back of his pants. He pulled it out and aimed. Madison followed the gun's sight and saw Lance running toward the car with the bag.

"No!" Madison knocked into Carsten's arm as the shot fired, sending the bullet spiraling into the woods.

"Madison! Those men tried to kill you!" Carsten shouted. The car sped away into the night, tires squealing. Carsten raised the gun and aimed again.

"Lance saved me in more ways than you'll know." Madison lowered her eyes. And Carsten lowered the gun.

~*~

Madison was silent on the way back to the

ranch. She sat with arms crossed against her chest, a subconscious protection of her battered heart. She stared straight ahead, not bothering to look at the passing scenery drenched in rich moonlight. Another night, under other circumstances, the landscape would be beautiful.

Tonight, it just seemed barren and empty.

Madison didn't flinch when Carsten coughed. It was the third sudden noise he'd made since leaving the warehouse in an effort to get her to talk. It wasn't working. She wouldn't let it. She had no idea what she was feeling right now. Except, blatant betrayal. Both by her father and the man she loved. Even if Carsten had lied to her for the right reasons, betrayal was still betrayal

She'd forgiven him in those dire moments in the warehouse. And while she was so grateful he'd come for her, it couldn't overshine the despair that her father hadn't.

She tried to pray, but couldn't find the words. God had rescued her tonight. Right? Or was she seeking Him, too, where He couldn't be found?

Maybe she was more alone than she thought.

She continued to stare aimlessly out the window. The tears threatened again. Finally, the road to the ranch loomed in sight, the front porch light shining a beacon in the darkness. She eagerly got out of the car, and waited for Carsten to unlock the front door. He paused, looking down at her, and she quickly averted her gaze.

She followed Carsten inside.

"Are you cold?" Carsten grabbed a blanket from the back of the couch without waiting for an answer. He draped it around her and helped her settle on the couch. Then he turned and began to make a fire.

Madison accepted the quilt and snuggled into the cushions. The fire started nicely, but she felt no heat. Her mind was too busy with other thoughts to process such things as senses.

Carsten sat on the cushion beside her and took her icy hand in his. He began briskly rubbing his palms over her hands in an effort to warm them. "You're cold. Maybe it's shock."

When Madison still refused to meet his gaze, Carsten snapped his fingers in front of her face. "Madison! Look at me!" Fear laced his tone.

Madison turned her head and looked into his eyes. The fire reflected in the limpid pools of blue, bringing a life to his eyes she knew was not reflected in her own. "You're safe now." Carsten wrapped an arm around Madison's shoulder, not letting go even when she didn't lean into his embrace. He smoothed her hair back with one hand. "I'm here."

Madison's stomach twisted. *You're here. But for how long?* She shrugged out of Carsten's embrace. Inside, she felt the walls in her heart building faster, brick by brick. She couldn't trust anyone to love her unconditionally.

Carsten was probably more trust worthy than most. But she couldn't take that risk. Not tonight.

Maybe not ever.

Carsten looked hurt at the abrupt dismissal of his touch, but Madison couldn't bring herself to feel anything.

The wall was almost complete.

"I need to talk to you."

Madison said nothing.

"This might not be the best time to tell you, but

in light of what happened between us the other day, I think that honesty is more important than timing right now."

Madison raised an eyebrow of interest, but kept staring into the flickering flames.

Carsten paused, and then released his final bombshell. "I paid for your ransom."

Her heart skipped a beat. She turned to face Carsten fully.

"I knew you would find out eventually and I wanted you to know the truth up front." He held up hands, offering a feeble smile. "He can be taught."

"How…" She stopped.

"I got the money together, Madison. It's done. How it came together isn't important."

She ducked her head as the news processed. A rush of guilt and sorrow flooded her entire being. Sorrow that Carsten, not her father, had paid for her rescue. And guilt that she'd assumed the worst in Carsten's motives toward her. He'd paid for her to be free.

As much as she wanted to let that light in and warm her, it couldn't pierce the intruding shadow of shame.

She was truly orphaned.

24

"She has to stay here, Mr. Lawrence. It's not safe. Those men are still out there, loose." Thanks to Madison's emotional reaction that had kept him from stopping them earlier that night at the scene.

Carsten stared out the kitchen window. The scenery he used to love so much did nothing to ease the storm in his heart. He swiped a hand over his face, thinking he hadn't been so exhausted in his entire career.

His client didn't seem any better rested. "And a fine job you did of keeping her protected the first time!"

Carsten bit his lip. He refused to get into an argument with the man. He'd blame Teddy's reaction on grief and adrenaline over the last few days' events, but in all honesty, the man had seemed more concerned about money than his daughter.

Which made Carsten even more determined to do what was best by her. He couldn't trust her dad to do the same.

"Mr. Lawrence, this is for the best. Madison won't run away again. She doesn't want a repeat of the past two days any more than we do." It wasn't as though the man had any money invested in her rescue. Carsten closed his eyes against the frustration building, not wanting to say something he'd regret. "I'll check in with you later." He pushed the off button on the cordless phone and tossed it on the couch He dreaded telling Madison she was being forced to stay at the ranch for a while longer. Lately she acted as if she'd rather be anywhere else. But he had to keep her safe. And not because her dad was paying him to.

At this point, he wouldn't accept a payment from Mr. Lawrence even if it was the only thing keeping him from being homeless.

He needed air. He wanted to race, like he always did to clear his mind when too much pressure consumed him. He wanted to mount Samson and fly like the wind over the hills. But now that Samson had a proud new owner, those days were gone.

Running a hand through his hair, he closed his eyes, desperate for sleep. The night had been long, too long. He checked his watch. It was three a.m. in New York. He knew Shan wouldn't be happy to hear from him at this hour.

He picked up the phone anyway.

~*~

"You sure know how to take a vacation." Shan's suitcase hit the floor with a thud in Madison's room.

Madison looked up in surprise from the book she was reading.

"Shan? What are you doing here?" Surprise and joy flooded Madison in equal measure. She tossed the book aside and stood.

Shan didn't answer, just opened her arms. The two friends embraced.

Tears streaked down Madison's face. "I've been

such a fool." To put it mildly. "This was all my fault."

"Don't be crazy." Shan cleared her throat against the uncharacteristic emotion evident in her voice. "I'm the one who tried to convince you to come out here. Neither one us had any clue what was going to happen. I'm just glad you're safe."

Madison sat down the edge of the bed, motioning for Shan to take a seat as well. "So did you come to try to cheer me up? "I'm basically under house arrest. And Carsten's been trying everything he can think of to get me to talk to him."

"Why won't you? The poor man's in love. Give him a break." Shan situated herself on the bed, leaning against the headboard and facing Madison. She tucked her legs underneath her.

In love? Hardly. More like paid to care.

She was the fool who loved him.

She averted her eyes, hoping Shan wouldn't see the truth. "He lied to me, Shan. I can't trust him."

"Sure, he might have withheld the truth about your dad hiring him, but he also took you in to protect you, and risked his own life coming to rescue you."

Madison raised her eyebrow. "Apparently, you've already heard his version."

Shan grinned sheepishly. "We did talk for a few minutes in the kitchen before I came upstairs. Is that information inaccurate?"

Madison plucked at a loose thread in the quilt underneath them. "No, it's true. He was willing to risk everything, and my father was willing to risk nothing." Now it was her turn to clear her throat.

Shan dipped her head until she caught

Madison's gaze. "Taking out your anger on Carsten isn't going to change your dad."

That one sunk in deep. Madison slipped off the bed and began to rearrange the items on the dresser. "That's not what I'm doing." She moved a bottle of lotion to the right side of the dresser, and then held a pair of earrings up to her ear. "Do these look good on me?"

"Girl, I wasn't born yesterday. Don't think you can change the subject that easily. But yes, I like the earrings a lot." Shan joined Madison at the dresser. "Can I borrow them?"

"Sure." Madison held them out. Anything to move on to a different topic.

"I'm kidding." Squirting some lotion into her palms, Shan rubbed the scented cream into her hands. "Just give Carsten a chance." Her voice softened. "He really cares for you, Madison."

"I don't know about that. I don't know much of anything right now." Madison shut the top dresser drawer firmly and met her friend's gaze in the mirror. "It's been a long few days, and I don't want to talk about it."

Shan held up both hands in surrender. "Of course. I just don't want you to make a mistake. I'm your friend, remember?"

And thank goodness for that. Madison relaxed. "I know you are. Thank you for coming out here." She paused. "Why are you here, again?"

Shan laughed. "Partly to cheer you up. But mostly because Carsten insisted I stay out here for precaution's sake. He thinks it's possible those men might try something again, and if that's the case, then I'm at risk as well. They've already broken into the office once before."

"So how long are you here?"

Shan shrugged. "I guess until the men are apprehended?"

Madison's spirits rose considerably. At least she wouldn't be stuck on the ranch alone. She remembered her reaction the day before when Carsten had given her that bit of news. She thought since she'd been rescued, she'd go back to New York and could resume her job and try to get over Carsten.

Much harder to do when on the same property as he was.

She hadn't exactly handled the piece of news well. "So, when do we eat?" Shan grinned, rubbing her flat stomach. "That airplane food did nothing for my appetite."

Madison shrugged. "Rita should have dinner on soon. The past few days she's been bringing me a tray up to my room. I haven't been exactly sociable." "Well, Ms. Social Butterfly is here now, so we will be eating in the dining room with the others. I want to meet me a real live cowboy." Shan raised her chin.

Madison wasn't sure if her friend was joking, or serious. But she wasn't about to argue with the look in Shan's eye.

~*~

"Rita, this was fabulous." Shan praised the older woman's cooking, dropping her napkin in her lap and shaking her head. "I think I just gained ten pounds."

Rita grinned at Shan's dramatics and thanked her for the compliment. "Nothing like good ol' home cooking, is there, dear?"

"We don't eat like this in the city. Most people in New York live on coffee alone. Except for Madison here, who'll occasionally scarf down a salad with her espresso." She nudged Madison in the elbow with her ribs.

"We'll fatten her up, yet." Rita winked at Madison over the top of her mug.

Madison forced a grin. It was beyond awkward sitting at the table for the meal. Luckily, Shan had kept a running conversation going with whoever would answer her.

The cowboys at the other end of the table couldn't keep their eyes off this new "city girl". She held the table captive with her antics and stories. Madison was grateful for that much. It was hard enough trying to avoid Carsten's piercing stare, much less participate in the conversation around her.

Her gaze darted to Carsten, almost against her will. Yep, still staring. She forced herself to look away.

"Who wants dessert?" Rita stood up to prepare the next course.

A herd of cowboys gleefully answered in unison.

"I might be able to find room for just a bite. I do have to watch this figure, you know." Shan winked at one of the men staring at her, and he blushed.

Madison grinned in spite of her dark mood. At least someone was enjoying themselves.

Rita served bread pudding moments later, and Madison busied herself in pretending to eat it. She hadn't had much of an appetite since she had gotten back to the ranch, and it was beginning to show. She had successfully hidden from Rita thus far by dumping the food out the window from her room and leaving the empty tray on the kitchen counter.

"Girl, you better eat that pudding. I saw what you had for dinner—exactly two bites of chicken and dumplings and three green beans!"

Madison should have known her luck would run out. Shan's eagle eye was a great asset for their design business, but not such a wonderful attribute when it concerned Madison's personal life. She picked up her spoon, wishing everyone would look away.

Carsten cleared his throat, and spoke for the first time since they sat down. "Leland, I saw a break in the fence in the north pasture this morning. I think you and a few others should ride down and fix it first thing tomorrow."

Leland nodded from his spot down the table. "Yes sir, boss." He had been promoted to foreman when Mitch had been fired.

Madison wondered if Carsten sensed her discomfort and had changed the subject purposely. She shrugged it off. It didn't matter if he was trying to rescue her. She no longer had a desire for a fairytale prince in her life. Charming or not, he was still just a man. And that meant he was eventually going to hurt her. He already had, in many ways.

She put down her spoon, her appetite too far gone to pretend anymore.

Shan scooted her chair back, looking eagerly to Carsten. "I want to see these horses you've been telling me about. I've never seen one up close."

"I'll be happy to give you a tour of the stables."

Carsten answered politely.

Shan turned to Madison. "Come on! I need you for moral support."

"They're not that bad." Madison mumbled, pushing back her own chair. It would take more energy trying to change Shan's mind than it would to just go ahead and accompany them. She knew what Shan was trying to do, and she was just as determined not to let it work. Two could play that game.

Shan linked arms with Madison and they followed Carsten out of the house. They walked along the yard in silence, Shan humming under her breath, and Madison staring at the ground, barely registering where she stepped.. Carsten stayed a few feet ahead Thankfully. She wanted this nightmare over so she could go home, recalibrate, and get on with her normal life. Whatever that looked like now.

They reached the stables and Carsten led the way to the first stall. "This is Champion." He began introducing Shan to each horse, making his way down the length of the barn.

Despite her earlier claim of needing moral support, Madison noticed Shan seemed perfectly comfortable with the animals. "This is Sasha. Madison rode her a few weeks ago, and she did great. Like a natural." Carsten spoke directly to Shan as if Madison wasn't even there.

Madison frowned, not knowing how to interpret that. She thought she detected sadness in his voice, and tried to ignore it. She fought back a twinge of pain at the happy memory of riding with him. And how he rescued her when her horse started running away.

He was always rescuing her.

"That's great, Madison!" Shan beamed at her friend. "You won't get me on one of these creatures. They sure are pretty but I enjoy being on the ground, thank you very much." She patted Sasha's neck. "No offense, lady."

Carsten chuckled. "Well, that's the tour."

"What about Samson?" Madison asked before realizing she was addressing Carsten directly, exactly as she had vowed not to.

Carsten ducked his head and said nothing. Shan looked confused.

Was he in the pasture? If that was the case, Carsten would have just said so. Not looked more like he had a another secret—

Realization dawned, and Madison's heart sank. "No…" she breathed. She hurried the last few feet to Samson's stall even though she could already see it was empty Her fears were confirmed when she looked over the wall into the desolate space. "Carsten…" Her voice cracked even as the truth registered. "You didn't."

"I did."

At his admission, her legs gave out, and she slid to a sitting position against the stall door.

Shan stood to the side, looking completely bewildered. "What's going on? Who is Samson? And where is he?"

Carsten ran a hand over his face, looking as if he were trying to regain his own composure. "I sold him." His voice was rough.

Tears slipped from Madison's eyes.

Shan looked between them both. "Why did you sell him"

Carsten's lack of response answered Shan's question.

"The money." Her expression fell..

Madison buried her face in her hands . It was all her fault. She felt so guilty. How many ways could she—or her family—wreck this man's life? All this time she'd been projecting her anger and frustration at her dad onto Carsten, when he'd done nothing but pick up all the broken pieces her dad left behind and keep them safe. Keep *her* safe.

Tears ran through the cracks between her fingers. "Carsten, I'm so sorry. You loved that horse."

Carsten knelt in the straw beside Madison, tugging her hands away from her face. She looked into his eyes, those same eyes that had beckoned her to dance in Germany what seemed like a lifetime ago.

Then he leaned close and whispered.. "I love you more."

25

Carsten held out the cordless phone.

"I don't want to talk to him." Madison turned her face. She protectively crossed her arms over her chest and shook her head.

Carsten sighed. The reaction was understandable, though perhaps a little immature. But her dad's betrayal had run deep. She wasn't ready—would she ever be? These days he wasn't sure.

"I'm sorry, Mr. Lawrence. Madison is still unavailable."

He watched as she slipped upstairs to her room and then he headed into the kitchen, where Rita was baking. He perched on a stool. "Yes sir. I suppose she still needs more time."

He caught Rita watching him from her post by the stove. She was stirring in a big pot, sending a delicious aroma wafting through the room.

"She'll come around." Her words carried confidence, but Carsten didn't feel so sure. He forced a grin and set the phone on the counter.

"Let me know when that's ready. It smells wonderful."

"You say that about everything." Rita waved him off, and Carsten went back into the living room. Madison was gone.

He felt the urge to pray—to surrender this entire

situation to someone with a little more control than he currently had.

But the words were as forced as his smile to Rita had been. "God, what do we do?" Silence.

Carsten crossed the room to sit on the hearth by the fireplace. His spirit was restless. He gazed up at the ceiling, knowing Madison's room wasn't far away. He could almost feel her up there, pacing the floor.

He wasn't the only one feeling a little anxious. It had been weeks since the kidnapping, and though Shan's presence helped, Madison was still not her usual self. She had barely spoken to Carsten since the incident in the stables.

Where he'd professed his love.

He groaned. Talk about bad timing. She hadn't responded, though the look in her eyes gave him hope that maybe she would in time.

He rested his chin on his fingertips and closed his eyes. God's protection of Madison during her kidnapping, and his swift finding of the angel and the diamond had given his faith a giant boost of late

Sadly, it seemed to do the opposite to Madison's.

He tried to pray again. *God, you know Madison better than I ever could. She needs to find peace and forgiveness. She is consumed by her bitterness. Only You can release that burden. Help her to see, Lord. Break down her walls.*

Carsten sat in silence for several moments, deep in thought and prayer. He felt a gentle stirring in his spirit, and for the first time in many years, truly believed that everything would turn out fine in the end. He saw a glimmer of light at the end of a very long tunnel.

~*~

Madison woke early the next morning. She couldn't get the words out of her head. They had played on repeat for weeks. "The girl's not even his real daughter... real daughter...real daughter..."

She stared at her reflection in the bathroom mirror. Who was she? She had to find out. Knowing had to be better than wondering, regardless of the outcome.

She slipped into her robe. Knotting it at the waist, she took the stairs down to the living room, searching for Carsten. He'd know how she could find out. She'd swing by the kitchen and ask Rita if he was out in the fields this morning.

"Rita!" Madison entered the kitchen full speed and then skidded to a stop at the sight of Carsten scrambling eggs at the stove. He looked over his shoulder and smiled.

Madison swallowed hard. The scene was way too homey. It was doing funny things to her stomach...and her heart. What would it be like to see him like this all the time? The thought entered her mind against her will, and she pushed it aside. She had too much to deal with before she entertained thoughts of Carsten. Of loving him back.

"I gave Rita the day off. I thought she could use a break." Carsten broke another egg and tossed the shell into the sink. He began stirring briskly the contents of a bowl. "Are you hungry? I know Shan will be."

He grinned, and for a moment, Madison could almost forget everything that had happened over the past month.

Almost.

Resolve stiffened her backbone. "I need a favor." She sat down on the bar stool.

Carsten kept his back to her as he worked over the skillet. "I'll do my best." With one hand, he flipped the eggs over with a spatula while grabbing a plate from the cabinet with the other.

Madison's stomach grumbled at the aroma. "I need you to find out if I'm adopted." The words left a bitter taste in her mouth.

Carsten looked up in surprise. "Why would you think you're adopted?" He turned the fire off and began scooping eggs onto the empty plate.

"Because of something I overheard Joseph and Lance saying."

Carsten didn't respond for several moments.

Madison waited. She knew what he was going to say and was already prepared with her answer

"Are you sure you want to know that, Maddie? Maybe it is best if you talked to your father first."

I've thought this through. I want to know before I speak to him again. You're the only one who can help me, Carsten. I know you have the resources to find out." She hesitated, knowing she was asking a lot, when she'd given very little back. "I'm just asking you to try."

Carsten slid the plate of eggs on the counter and walked over to stand directly in front of her. He looked deeply into her eyes, and slid his hand under her hair to cup her neck. "You know I can't deny you anything." His voice was husky, and warmth ran down Madison's spine.

She closed her eyes against the touch of his hand

and then gently ducked out of his grip. "Thank you."

She tried to smile, but the effort failed miserably. "I'll go tell Shan breakfast is ready."

She left the room quietly.

~*~

Carsten watched Madison leave, trying to fight the dark cloud of misery that threatened to settle over him. She looked way too cute first thing in the morning, and the sight of her with messy hair and a robe made him think about the future. He wanted her in it, even though at this point it seemed hopeless to even consider the possibility. Madison was gone. Her body was still on the Running R ranch, but her spirit, her spunk and personality that had drawn him to her like a moth to flame, had disappeared into a hardened shell. Could God even crack it?

A sharp burning smell suddenly permeated the air, and Carsten quickly grabbed for the burners and turned them off. The woman showed up with a single heartfelt plea, and he almost set the kitchen on fire. He had to distance himself, and wait. It was out of his hands.

"You're in control, God. Help me to stop trying to take over." Carsten breathed the prayer that had gotten him through the past several weeks and then began to make toast. There was nothing else he could do.

~*~

The next few days passed in a blur for Madison.

She had developed somewhat of a routine. Now that she had Shan's help, the two got to work on the decorating project. Madison was determined to fulfill her duty as a designer.

Whether her initial job offer had been real was irrelevant. She needed something to do, a goal of some kind. She hated staying in a place without pulling her weight. Since Rita had the cooking and cleaning under control, Madison and Shan put all their energy into decorating. Carsten wouldn't let them leave the house for supplies, but they made do with what he and Madison had bought on their previous trip, along with a few other creatively resourced items. Slowly, the house began to take shape.

"You girls are doing a great job." Carsten stated one afternoon as he walked into the downstairs bathroom. Shan was kneeling on the floor, painting the baseboards, while Madison stood on a ladder, stenciling a border.

Shan thanked Carsten for the compliment. Madison smiled stiffly, not looking up from her work. Carsten waited in the doorway. At his sigh, she turned and saw him walk away, his strong shoulders slightly drooped. The sight twisted her stomach, but she turned back to the design and kept stenciling.

"Girl, I hope you know what you're doing," Shan muttered.

Silence was Madison's only response.

The days kept passing, and Madison still refused to talk to her father, though he made several attempts at communication. She finally finished the house. Every wall had been painted, along with a fresh coat of white for the trim. Accent pillows and rugs were scattered throughout the house, along with new lighting and several pots of strategically placed plants and flowers. Every room was complete, except for the master bedroom. Madison couldn't bring herself to go inside it. That was where Carsten had taken to sleeping, and she wouldn't let herself get that close to him. It seemed too intimate.

Each time she passed the room, her traitorous mind would entertain thoughts of what it would be like to marry Carsten and live on the ranch permanently. Carsten never asked why Madison and Shan hadn't redone the room. Madison figured he understood, and probably also preferred not to talk about it. It was too painful to think of what might have been.

What possibly still could be, if she got her life figured out. But how could she love Carsten when she wasn't sure who she was? She had nothing to give right now, and he had already given so much. It wasn't fair to him.

Madison also was beginning to grow weary hearing Shan's complaints about "farm life". Though she was ready to leave the ranch and the emotional turmoil of being around Carsten every day, she personally had little desire to dive back into the smog of the city. But Shan was more than ready to return. "We're going to be here forever," Shan whined. "I need Starbucks!"

Each time, Madison would say, "You'll be home before you know it."

Shan never knew how much it cost Madison to say those words. She still wasn't sure where her home truly was. With her father in Georgia? At her apartment in New York? At work? Her heart cried an answer she didn't want to acknowledge— with Carsten.

The wandering sensation in her spirit only magnified the night the phone rang. Rita was just clearing the supper dishes from the table when Carsten came back into the dining room, a grave expression on his face. He asked to speak to Madison alone.

With rattling nerves, Madison followed him into the living room. She took her usual position on the couch and waited for the inevitable. She could tell by his face what he had discovered. Even so, she wasn't prepared for the blow of his words.

"My connection just phoned. He found your file. Madison, you were adopted when you were three months old."

An icy film crept over her heart. All the years of wondering why she wasn't good enough, of fighting her father for freedom, of feeling as if she didn't fit in, suddenly made sense. But pain came with the clarity, striking pain that lingered deep in her soul.

Carsten cleared his throat, but she couldn't look at him. Couldn't take the sympathy she knew would hover in his eyes. Could she accept the fact that this would always be a part of her? It would create her identity. The cold truth changed everything. Doubts flogged her memories. Did any of it count now? Had any of it been real?

Madison lifted a trembling hand to her heart. How could they have kept such a thing from her all these years?? She closed her eyes as grief threatened to consume her.

No wonder her dad hadn't paid her ransom.

He'd already purchased her once.

"Maddie?"

She jerked, opening her eyes, yet still avoiding Carsten's gaze. "Thank you for finding out for me." Her words were stiff, and she stood awkwardly, feeling foreign in her own skin. Was it better to know, after all? Yes. Maybe. He had tried to warn her.

It was too late now.

She caught Carsten's nod of acknowledgement out of the corner of her eye, and blinked hard to keep back the tears. She wanted a hug. But her heart closed, wrapping around itself in a protective shield.

She wouldn't get hurt again.

26

Carsten threw himself into his work. He spent every waking moment outside helping the ranch hands or inside on his laptop computer. He sent emails daily, spreading the word to various contacts about Joseph and Lance. As much as he wanted Madison to stay at the ranch, he hated the idea that her kidnappers were still loose. He knew vengeance was the Lord's, but at times, he fought the temptation to take over.

His mornings and nights were filled with constant prayer for Madison, as well as for himself, while his days were spent laboring. He had become as much a worker as the rest of his staff, and he sensed a new level of respect from each of them.

Even though several of the cowboys showed a genuine interest in Madison and Shan, they kept their distance. They had all been within hearing range when Carsten ordered Mitch to leave months before. None of them wanted a repeat of that German rage.

Carsten's spiritual life strengthened to the point that he could honestly say he wanted what was best for Madison, even if that meant not being with her. He wanted her to forgive her father and move on with her life. Of course, he also wanted to marry her and have a dozen children. But he was leaving that part up to God.

He couldn't help but notice Madison's distance from all things spiritual. She wasn't even bowing her head at the table during grace. He would simply have to pray for her in that area, as well.

His cellphone rang one cold afternoon in October. He shifted the strand of barbed wire to his other hand and dug the phone from his jacket pocket, fumbling through his thick gloves.

"Good news."

The voice on the other end was that of a co-worker from Angel Enterprises. Carsten held the phone against his ear with his shoulder and kept pulling the wire taunt. "I'm listening."

"I have a Mr. Joseph Styles in custody in New York City."

Carsten's grip let go of the wire and it sprung back in protest. His breath caught in his throat. One down. "What about Lance?"

The line was silent. Carsten gripped the phone, straining to hear through the static of the connection. Had Lance managed to escape?

"That is not such good news. Joseph is responsible for his brother's death."

Carsten bowed his head as the news registered. Joseph had killed Lance. Somehow, he wasn't surprised. The man was wicked, and his brother had been weak. Still, how could someone murder his own brother?

These were the days his job was hard. How would the news affect Madison? Though Lance had been the one to kidnap her, he had also saved her. She obviously felt grateful; she had saved the man's life in return. Now Carsten understood on a fresh level why she'd stopped him that night. She knew more about those dynamics than he had in the heat of the rescue.

She'd made the right decision, and had saved him from a lot of regret.

"My boys apprehended Joseph at the border," the agent continued. "He was trying to sneak into Mexico. Let's just say he did not succeed."

Carsten breathed a sigh of relief as the weight of the words sunk in. The danger was past. That meant that Madison and Shan were free to go back to New York City.

His stomach tightened at the thought. Was this a test from God, his chance to prove that he loved Madison enough to let her go? Could do it? His strength faltered.

"Thank you for calling."

"I'll be in touch." The line went dead.

Carsten stayed outside until the sun set. He knew the sooner he went inside, the sooner reality would begin, and Madison would disappear from his life.

Forever.

~*~

Rita made a huge farewell dinner. Madison couldn't see her plate for all the food that covered it. Shan ate heartily, excited to be heading back to the city. She kept muttering about coffee and concrete. But it was all Madison could do to keep her dinner down. She didn't know what she felt. She was more numb than emotional. The coldness that had sunk in with Carsten's announcement of her past had settled into a chilling ache that wouldn't go away. She pushed the steak around on her plate while Shan dished up seconds.

"I'm sure gonna miss this good cooking," she told Rita. "I wish I could get a to-go box."

The others just smiled at her rambling. The air was thick with tension, and Shan was the only one who seemed oblivious. Even the cowboys picked up on it. They ate in silence then went back to work.

"When does your flight leave?" Rita asked from across the table, for Madison's ears only.

She met her gaze briefly. "Nine a.m." She dropped her napkin over her plate.

Rita nodded. "I'll make you a special breakfast."

Madison smiled. The older woman showed her love not through affection, but through food. She couldn't turn down the gesture. "I'd appreciate that."

Carsten pushed his chair back abruptly. "Thank you for a delicious dinner, Rita." He left the room.

Madison wondered what his plans were. Now that she and Shan were leaving, would he go back to Germany? Or make his home at the ranch? He fit so well in both places. Madison's heart stirred for the first time in weeks. She wished he would stay at the ranch. She felt better knowing he was on the same continent. She didn't have a tangible reason why except for the longing in her heart that would always be denied.

After the dishes were cleared, Shan excused herself, saying she needed to use the phone now that it was safe to talk freely of her whereabouts. Madison watched her friend leave, knowing that they would both have a lot of calls to make once they got back to the office. Their clients were probably feeling abandoned. She could understand the concept.

Pushing aside the bitterness, Madison winced at the thought of all the work that lay in front of them. Hopefully their business wouldn't be permanently affected by their extended leave of absence.

She wandered into the living room, subconsciously looking for Carsten. She saw at a glance that the door to the master bedroom was shut, and she wondered if he had gone to bed early in order to avoid a goodbye. That didn't seem like him. Carsten was polite, almost to a fault. He would be more likely to sacrifice his own emotional well-being in order to do the right thing, rather than take the easy way out.

Madison stood in the center of the living room, staring into the dark fireplace. The wind howled outside, rattling the windows, and it sent a chill down her back. She busied herself making a fire, trying not to think of the fact that it would be for the last time on the Running R.

Grabbing her favorite blanket, she curled up on the floor in front of the fire and watched the flames dance. Her body warmed instantly, but her heart felt frozen solid. She was trapped, a prisoner of her own will.

Laying her head against the cool of the bricks, Madison closed her eyes, listening to the fire crack and hiss as it devoured the wood. Time passed, and she slept.

~*~

Carsten lay in bed with eyes wide open. He had gone to his room hours before, too emotionally and physically drained to face a goodbye with Madison.

He would put off the inevitable until the morning, when he would drive both of the girls to the airport.

He rolled over on his side and closed his eyes, willing sleep to come. Being awake was too painful. He tried to pray, but his racing thoughts got in the way. Restless, he swung his legs over the side of the bed and stood. Maybe a glass of water would help.

He made his way down the hall in the dark, not wanting to disturb Rita, who slept in the room across the way. A flickering light from the living room caught his attention, and he frowned. Was that a fire? He quickened his step.

Dull embers burned in the fireplace. To his surprise, he found Madison curled up, asleep on the floor near the hearth, wrapped up in a blanket and still wearing her clothes from dinner. Her mouth hung open a little, and her tangled blonde hair covered half of her face.

Carsten smiled in spite of his emotional overload. She was so gorgeous. Did she have any idea? He watched the steady rise and fall of her chest as she slept, a peaceful expression on her face. Probably the first peace she'd had in months. His heart ached at the thought of all she'd been through. To be stalked, taken across the country, kidnapped, and then to find out she was adopted...it was too much for anyone to process. No wonder she felt lost.

Quietly, he crept over to Madison's spot on the floor and brushed the hair off her face. She stirred, moving her arms out in a stretch and then curling back up into a new position. Carsten tugged the blanket over her shoulders and then sat a few feet away, resting his back against the bricks.

He watched her as time passed. The clock

became his enemy. He felt completely content, sitting and studying his sleeping angel. He never wanted the night to end.

He breathed a prayer of gratitude at the chance to observe her before she walked out of his life forever. The thought twisted his stomach. How could he stand to let her go? To watch her leave...and probably never come back. What reason would she have ever to return? Madison had experienced nothing positive on his ranch. Only deception, danger, and tears.

Though, there had been some good moments, he had to admit. He closed his eyes as the memories flashed behind his eyelids. Her first horseback ride, the way she enjoyed herself yet tried to hide it. Shopping in town...that little black dress.

He groaned and opened his eyes. No sense going back to that fateful night. Carsten turned his gaze back to the one who unknowingly owned his heart, and memorized her features.

~*~

Madison woke abruptly. Where was she? She stiffened in alarm then sat up fast.

"You're OK." Carsten's voice registered first, then his gentle squeeze of her hand. He released it almost as fast as he'd picked it up.

She sat back, pulling the blanket up over her body. "What time is it?"

He checked his watch. "Almost three. You fell asleep."

"Madison pushed her hair away from her face in a tired motion, feeling groggy and like the weight of the world rested on her shoulders. But she was free—why was she still heavy? She began to stand. "Why didn't you wake me up?"

"I wanted to spend time with you."

She stopped. "I was asleep."

"I take what I can get." His sad smile matched everything she felt inside.

She remained seated, though she shifted into a new position, trying to convince herself to stand up and walk away.

Easier said than done. She inhaled deeply. "I should go. My plane leaves in a few hours. I have to finish packing."

Carsten nodded, looking at his hands. "I know, *mein angel*. I'm very much aware."

Something inside her shifted at Carsten's soft admission. Like a brick coming down. She struggled to put it back. She couldn't afford to feel anything, not now when she was almost safely back in the chaos of New York, far away from the countryside and a certain foreign man who had stolen her heart.

Carsten reached out tentatively, gripping Madison's hand in his. "I need to say something to you."

Madison began to withdraw her hand, knowing instinctively where the conversation was going. She couldn't handle it. "No—" Her protest fell on deaf ears.

"You own a piece of my heart, Maddie. You always will, no matter how far away you go. You first staked a claim on a snowy night in Germany, and you further brand me every time you look at me the way you do. The way you did."

Madison stopped trying to pull away and closed

her eyes, tears streaming down her cheeks as he continued. His words were like a balm to her heart, but the initial application stung and made her want to jerk away.

She needed to hear this. But oh, it hurt.

"I know you're scared, I know you need time and space, and that's why I'm not going to push you. Or follow you. I want what's best for you."

His grip on her hands tightened, and Madison opened her eyes to find Carsten swallowing hard. A tear slipped from the corner of his eye, and he pressed a kiss into her palm.

"I'm going to be here. If you feel lost in the city, you have a home here, with me. Please remember that."

Madison nodded, knowing she could never return to the ranch. Not unless she was ready to fully commit. Would she ever be healed enough to do so?

She couldn't stand crushing the little hope to which Carsten seemed to be clinging. So she stayed silent.

"I love you, Maddie. I love you in a way that I'll never love anyone else, no matter what the future brings."

Tears flowed freely down her face, and Carsten drew Madison into his embrace. She hugged him back, clinging fiercely, knowing that the moment she let go, her fairytale would end.

27

Madison didn't sleep that night. After her conversation with Carsten, she went and lay in her bed until dawn, the events of the past several months running through her mind like a record on repeat.

When the sun began streaming through the edges of the curtain, spraying patterns of light on the hardwood floor, she got up. She went through the motions of getting ready for the day, feeling as if she were in daze. When she had procrastinated as long as possible, she dragged her suitcases down the stairs. Rita was putting the final touches on breakfast, which smelled heavenly.

Though the food tasted delicious, there was a dark cloud looming over the breakfast table. Even Shan felt the tension this time, and rambled on in an attempt to lighten the mood, cracking jokes about "getting back to civilization." Madison couldn't determine exactly how she felt. One glance into Carsten's piercing blue eyes and she knew what was in his heart. Rita tried to put on a cheery face but even her best efforts seemed forced and unnatural.

Finally, the clock chimed eight a.m. It was time to leave for the airport. Shan and Madison argued with Carsten, trying to convince him to let them take a bus, but he would have none of it. He loaded their luggage into the Jeep, and motioned for them to make their goodbyes. Shan hugged Rita briefly, an act that caused the woman's eyes to open wide with surprise, but she seemed to enjoy the attention nonetheless.

Shan headed for the Jeep, while Madison turned to face Rita. "I don't know what to say."

Rita nodded, lips pursed. "You'll be back."

Madison didn't have the heart to argue with her, so she just held out her arms. The two women embraced, and Madison felt a tear drip onto her neck. "I'll be seeing you." Rita turned abruptly back to the house.

Feeling as if her limbs were made of lead, Madison climbed into the front of the vehicle. She buckled in, and Carsten started the engine. She kept her head turned away to hide the tears. Her heart screamed at her through a flurry of emotions, and Madison knew if she stopped to listen, she'd never make it out of town. She turned the dial on the radio and cranked up the volume. They rode to the airport to the tune of an old country song.

The drive took up a solid half hour, though to Madison it sped by as quickly as the passing scenery outside her window. Carsten parked the car in the short-term lot and ushered Shan and her inside the small airport, while somehow managing all the luggage. Madison's heart swelled as she watched him check their bags and hoist the carry-ons onto the security belt. He was always such a gentleman. Her stomach fluttered and she wondered if she was doing the right thing.

Carsten flashed a badge and was able to accompany them to the gate. With each step, a war raged inside Madison. Did she listen to her head, or her heart? Her mind was screaming at her to protect, to withdraw, to run away, to avoid pain at all costs. Her heart was tempting her to stay, seducing her with visions of a life with Carsten, safely tucked into his arms for the remainder of her life. But it couldn't be.

She was too broken.

"That's us!" Shan announced. Madison shook her head to clear it. She hadn't even heard the announcement over the intercom. Willing herself to pay attention, she followed Shan toward the gate, flight ticket in hand. Shan went first, surrendering her ticket to the attendant and practically bouncing up and down with anticipation.

Madison was slower to follow, her feet like weights. She handed the woman her ticket, which the woman stamped and handed back. "Have a nice flight," she cooed through a layer of lipstick.

Madison shoved the pass in her back pocket and turned to face Carsten, who handed her the remaining carry-on duffel bag. His Adam's apple bobbed in his throat, and Madison knew he was fighting back tears. Her mind raced back to the night before, where they held each other near the fire. He had cried freely then, and she knew if he wasn't in public, he would again.

"Thanks for everything." It seemed to understated. But she wasn't sure what else to say. She fumbled with the strap of her duffel instead.

Carsten nodded. "It was my pleasure." His gaze met hers and said everything his voice didn't. *Don't go.*

Madison took a deep breath. She felt as if all the air had been sucked out of the room. Could she really get on the plane and leave? She wanted to trust him, she wanted to step fearlessly into the future and believe that they truly had something special, that he wouldn't hurt her like her father had... but she couldn't.

There had been too many lies, too many secrets, and too many emotional upheavals in too short a time for her to take that step right now. If she tried, and he betrayed her like her dad did—she'd never recover.

Her heart remained locked, impenetrable behind her carefully constructed wall.

She glanced away, and the moment was gone. She boarded the plane, stubbornness and pain denying her a glance back.

~*~

Carsten watched from the window as Madison's plane taxied down the runway. His soul felt like it was dying, but he forced himself not to give in to the misery. He watched through a misty gaze as the plane lifted off, carried Madison away from him. She was really gone. He accepted the fact, partly because he trusted God and His ultimate plan, and partly because he had no other choice.

He waited by the window for a moment longer and then turned away. He knew this was goodbye, not because he couldn't find her if he wanted to; his resources and connections guaranteed him that much, but because she didn't want to be found. He'd promised he wouldn't follow her.

He needed coffee. He headed to the airport restaurant, and bought the biggest cup of black coffee the café offered. It cleared his head, but did little for his heart. He sipped it slowly as he wandered through the gift shop, picking up magazines without really seeing the titles and flipping aimlessly through postcards on the turnstile. He had no reason to be here still, it wasn't as if Madison was coming back. He just couldn't face the ranch without her. Once he got home, it would be official. The ranch wouldn't be the same without her smile, her sarcastic humor, her artistic touch on everything throughout his home…

Carsten jammed his fingers through his hair. What on earth had possessed him to let the woman redecorate his entire house? He would never be able to turn a single corner without encountering something she had created. It would be torture. *You didn't know you would fall in love…*His conscience tormented him.

He had to go back to Germany. It was the only answer. He dropped his lukewarm coffee in the nearest trashcan and headed for the ticket counter.

He would leave tomorrow.

28

Ticket in pocket, Carsten drove home, his mind and heart competing over how to feel. He was trying to have faith. He was trying to trust that everything would turn out well in the end.

But the fact that Madison was on a plane that was by now hundreds of miles away cast a shadow of doubt over his belief.

His cellphone rang, and he dug it out of his pocket while keeping his eyes on the road.

"Carsten, this is Teddy Lawrence. We need to talk."

Carsten sighed, and fought the temptation to drive the Jeep right off the road. Could this day get any worse? He braced himself for another verbal assault. "Yes sir."

"I feel that I have some explaining to do. At the very least, I owe you an apology."

This time, he almost ran off the road with surprise. He jerked back into his lane and gripped the phone tighter. "What did you say, sir?" There was a long pause. "I feel that I reacted badly in the face of pressure. I took out my frustrations over, well, many different things and for that, I'm sorry."

Carsten didn't know what to say. It didn't matter, because Teddy was still talking.

"I have no justifiable excuse for my behavior other than stress, and I felt that I should make things up to you. You should expect a gift delivery sometime tomorrow."

Carsten swallowed hard. "That's not necessary."

Teddy's voice was stiff. "Yes, it is."

He decided not to argue. From the sound of his tone, it was evident that making the phone call was hard enough for Teddy. Carsten didn't want to make it worse for him.

He bit back all the things he wanted to unload on the man, and forced a smile he hoped he'd hear. "Thank you, sir."

"You're welcome. I hope you enjoy it. You're not the only one with connections, you know."

Carsten snorted. "I never assumed."

He disconnected the call, and his mind wandered. What had caused the sudden change of heart in Mr. Lawrence? Carsten decided not to question a blessing, and instead, praised God for the surprise. He didn't know what tomorrow would hold, but He did know that it was in God's hands. That would have to be enough.

Rita was quiet when he got back to the ranch. Carsten told her about his plans to leave for Germany the next day. She said she understood, but her eyes glistened. Carsten felt a twinge of guilt over leaving her. He knew it had to be hard on Rita to see Madison and Shan go. She had shown her love for the girls in her own way throughout their visit. He knew she had secretly hoped that things would turn out differently for him and Madison, but then again, so had he.

"I'll cook you a special dinner." She bustled off to the kitchen. Carsten smiled sadly. He would miss her, as well as her cooking. He thought of the bachelor pad awaiting him in Germany and almost changed his mind about the trip. But one glance into the living room cleared his mind.

Madison had outdone herself in her design. Never had the space appeared so large and inviting. He saw the fireplace from the corner of his eye, and remembered the previous night where he and Madison had sat and talked. It already felt like a lifetime ago.

There was no doubt about it. He had to leave. It was simply too painful. He gave the room one last sweeping glance and turned down the hall to his room. It, too, reminded him of Madison, not because of her decorating, but because the lack of it. She had skipped this room entirely, and Carsten knew it had been done on purpose. Did she feel the same way about him when she looked inside the master bedroom? Did she secretly wish that she could decorate it to her own tastes and occupy it with him as his wife?

Evidently, she didn't, or she wouldn't have left.

Carsten ran a hand through his hair and moaned. He had to get away before he went insane. He grabbed his cowboy hat off the dresser and shoved it on his head before leaving the room. The back door slammed behind him as he rushed to the stables as if he were being chased by a ghost.

He supposed in many ways, he was.

~*~

He slept later than he meant to. The sun streamed in golden layers through the window when Carsten finally opened his eyes after a restless night's sleep. He yawned and contemplated staying in bed. Determined not to wallow in his misery, he finally stood and stretched.

A loud whinny from outside caught his attention, and he paused, arms still above his head. He listened, wondering if he was dreaming. The whinny came again, and it sounded familiar.

Carsten pulled back the curtain and stared. Samson stood on the front lawn, munching on a block of hay. His reins were tied loosely to the front porch railing. The beautiful horse looked up at the movement in the window and whinnied again.

Feeling like a little kid on Christmas morning, Carsten pulled on the nearest pair of pants and shirt and ran outside, still barefoot. The ground was cold beneath his feet but he didn't care.

"Samson! How did you—" He stopped as Teddy Lawrence's words from the day before sank in. *You should expect a gift delivery sometime tomorrow...*

The man knew how to apologize.

Carsten untied the rope from the rail and clucked softly to Samson. "This way. You're home now." He led the stallion to his old stall, making sure he was safely put away and cared for before returning back to the house to grab his boots.

His heart full of gratitude, he planned a carefree day of riding, his flight to Germany no longer a priority.

"Rita! You won't believe it!"

The day was turning out to be much better than he had imagined.

~*~

She had never been so miserable in her life.

Madison went through the motions of her everyday work schedule, feeling as if she had been taken over by a robot. She saw what she did, and she knew she was doing it, but her inner drive and ambition was missing. She wasn't herself, and it was beginning to show. She knew from the curious looks Shan gave her, the way their new receptionist tip-toed around as though she were afraid of offending, and the way that her clients asked Shan softly spoken questions when they thought Madison couldn't hear.

She noticed, but found it hard to care. She was feeling just that way when Shan burst into her office one chilly December morning.

"I found the garland!" She was wearing it draped around her neck like a boa. Posing like a supermodel, Shan stood framed in the doorway, draped in greenery and looking way too cheerful for Madison's taste.

"Congratulations," she mumbled.

Shan frowned. "Don't make me bring over the mistletoe."

Madison smirked.

Shan threatened her with the piece of greenery. "I know I'm not who you want to kiss, but don't think I won't do it! Girl, you've got to smile. It's almost Christmas!"

"Trust me, I know. And I have no family to spend it with."

"And that is completely your own fault."

Madison raised her eyebrows at her friend's bluntness. Shan held out her arms in defense. "Don't look at me that way. I'm just telling you the truth. I know for a fact your father has been trying to contact you for almost three months now. If you choose to spend Christmas without family, it's your own choice."

Madison's temper flared, but then she lost all energy and deflated like a balloon. "I don't even know who my real family is." She sank into the desk chair.

Shan sighed and came over to perch on the side of the desk. "Does it matter?" Her voice was gentle though her words were piercing. "What I mean is, you have family, Madison. Why does it matter that it was a delivery through a piece of paper rather than flesh and blood? Your father loves you. Your mother did, too. I know that from the pictures I've seen and the stories I've heard. You carry a lot of bitterness, but I know the love is there on both sides. Give your dad a chance. It's almost Christmas."

Madison shrugged, feeling the tears well up. She turned away abruptly. She knew from experience over the past few weeks that once she started crying, it took a long time to stop.

"And don't forget, I'm your family, too. And I know we're not related by blood." Shan grinned and held her dark complexioned arm next to Madison's fair skinned one.

A smile finally broke through to the surface, and Madison hugged her friend. "Thank you." It was all she could say at the moment, but it was enough.

Shan returned the hug and then wrapped Madison up in a big roll of tinsel. "Time to decorate!"

They turned on the stereo and listened to a local station that was playing Christmas music through the month of December.

Shaking her hips to "Jingle Bells" while tacking

tinsel to her desk, Madison felt considerably light-hearted. It was almost enough to make her want to call her father.

Almost.

29

Carsten spent the next two weeks praying like he had never prayed before. He prayed in the mornings while it was still dark out. He prayed while he worked on the land and went for his daily rides on Samson. He prayed before every meal and while he was in the shower. He prayed while falling asleep in bed. At first, he prayed because he wanted to change God's mind about his relationship with Madison. But the more he prayed, the more he realized God was changing his heart, rather than the other way around. And he was truly content for the first time in a long time.

Being that close to God made everything seem different, more purposeful, somehow. Carsten saw the ranch in a new light. He saw nature and all of God's creation as a miracle. His spirit felt satisfied.

That didn't mean he didn't still think about Madison. He couldn't forget her if he tried. He still pictured her blonde hair hanging down her back as she rode ahead of him on Sasha, and dreamt of her fiery eyes and musical laugh. But he had arrived at a new place in his life, a place of trust that he had never before imagined possible.

The trip to Germany had been put off indefinitely. Rita was grateful. She showed him her gratitude through mountains of food and a sparkling house. He was glad she was happy. He knew he was like a son to her, and she didn't need any more loss in her life. He was content on the ranch. He had his work, his land, his horse, and most importantly, his relationship with God.

Occasionally, he prayed and asked God if he was doing the right thing. He still fought the temptation to jump on the next flight to New York and sweep Madison off her feet. But every time he prayed about it, he felt an urging in his spirit to wait. God never revealed more than that one, single word: Wait.

He was beginning to hate the word, but eventually he decided that the right thing in the wrong timing was still the wrong thing. So he forced himself to be patient, working harder than he ever worked before. The ranch took on a new shape. Any repair that needed to be done, he found and repaired it.

He finally backed off when his foreman approached him one evening, worried about being worked out of a job. After that, Carsten occupied himself with details of a plan on how to get Madison back to the ranch. But each time he tried to work through the details, conviction once again struck his heart, and he wavered in the space between trust and doubt. He knew God had a plan for his life.

But he feared it might not include Madison.

One morning, while riding through the north pasture checking fence lines, he felt a change in his spirit. He pulled Samson to a halt. "God?" He waited, holding his breath, hoping. Was it time? Was this his sign?

There was the same urging in his spirit, a gentle command. But this time it was a different word. Still wait, but with it, something more. He listened harder. *Trust.*

He smiled. He could do that. With newly strengthened faith, and a hope that threatened to take his breath away, Carsten made a decision to put his trust into action. He put Samson in the barn and went to clean up. Then he headed into town. He had an errand to run. What would come of it, he had no idea. That was up to God. Carsten would just do his own part.

He would trust.

~*~

Madison felt restless. The cheery atmosphere of her office did little to ease her mind. She stared at the sparkly tinsel on her desk until it started to blur. Shan had already left for the day, declaring Christmas Eve a national holiday and demanding an early out. Madison hadn't argued. If she were in circumstances other than her own, she'd have felt the same way.

She needed to get out. There would be no more phone calls or clients today. Most people had taken the day, or even the previous week, off from work.

Madison tried to rein in the negativity and decided some fresh air would clear her mind. She bundled up in her pink pea coat and matching cashmere gloves and scarf. She locked up the office and set out at a brisk pace, content to walk and watch.

Christmas time in New York was evident at every light post and corner. Wreaths, garland, and mistletoe decorated the city. She kept walking, observing the people passing by. Stores were closing their doors and turning off lights, ready to go home to a fancy feast with their families.

She passed by a street musician, playing "Deck the Halls" on his harmonica, and dropped some change in his open case. He nodded his thanks and switched to "Jingle Bells".

Madison walked for blocks, not worrying about the setting sun or the crowds on the street. There was a magical quality in the air, brought by the holiday season, and she felt safe wrapped inside it.

It reminded her of Germany.

She rubbed her hands together through her gloves. It was getting colder. She looked up at the sky just as the clouds released their snowflake prisoners, sending a flurry spiraling downward like powdered sugar dusting over a cake. She held her face to the moisture for a moment; breathing in the fresh, clean scent.

Even though she enjoyed the snow, she wanted to get warm. She looked up the street for a taxi and saw none. Walking one more block ahead, she found herself in front of a small chapel. Lanterns glowed in the windows, offering a safe, warm haven, and Madison stepped inside.

Standing in the foyer, she dusted the snow off her coat and unwound her scarf. Pushing the gloves in her coat pocket, she walked a few steps and stopped short at the beauty of the church. A tall ceiling accented by stained glass windows caught her artistic eye, and she stepped quietly down the aisle. The church was empty except for a few people bowed in prayer in the front pews.

She slid into a row in the back and sat reverently. Her stomach clenched, and she realized that it had been way too long since she had prayed. She realized that the wall she had built protectively around her heart had blocked out not only her friends and family, but also her Lord.

Madison bowed her head. She didn't know where to start, and a tear dripped onto her lap. She sniffed and tried again. "God..." She began to sob.

Not wanting to draw the attention of the people in the front, Madison covered her face with her hands to muffle the sound. The tears released the pent up anger and bitterness inside, and when she was done, she felt purged.

Raising her gaze, she noticed the picture on the window closest to her. It was that of Jesus on the cross, arms stretched wide. She felt for the first time that those arms were opening wide just for her, for salvation as well as for comfort and love and security. Those arms were the only ones she truly needed.

Regardless of the dynamics of her family, she was loved. Fully, deeply, wholly loved.

She whispered her thoughts to God, sending a heartfelt prayer of repentance to the heavens. She knew in her spirit she was forgiven, and she was also just as certain that she would have to forgive.

First herself and then her father.

"It's hard." Madison whispered. "I have so much to learn about trust." She looked once more to the cross on the colored panes, and took a deep breath. "But I forgive him."

Her wall cracked.

She tried a smile. It felt sincere. "I really do." And then the wall dismantled piece by piece.

Madison knew she still had many things to

discuss with her dad. There were questions that desperately needed answering. Why didn't he tell her she was adopted? Why didn't he make time for her when she was growing up?

The answers were irrelevant. Teddy Lawrence was her dad, the father that God provided for her, and she intended from this point forward to be grateful and stop harassing herself with doubts and insecurities.

"Thank you, Lord, for the snow, and for bringing me into this chapel, and most importantly, for being there with arms open wide."

Madison sat silently in the church for a moment longer until she felt her heart would simply burst. It was Christmas Eve, and she had a gift for her father—her unconditional love. She had to talk to him, right away. Maybe it wasn't too late to get a flight down to Georgia for Christmas day.

She stood from the pew, eager to make her plans. As she pushed open the heavy doors and walked outside into the snowy night, an idea dawned. She glanced at her watch. It would work if she hurried.

30

The frozen ground crunched under Madison's boots as she walked purposefully across the pasture. During the long talk she'd had with her father, he'd told her that he'd gotten Samson back for Carsten. She had a hunch he'd be out here riding. Sure enough, Madison could just make out the familiar Stetson at the bottom of the hill. She squinted. He was sitting in the saddle, gazing out across the barren fields.

Something stirred in Madison's heart. She tried to keep from running to him, but as she got closer, she found herself at a jog. The cold air pierced her lungs and burned her nose, but she didn't care. The sight of the man in front of her warmed her heart.

A sudden doubt slowed her pace. From his hunched shoulders and vacant stare, he appeared upset. She stopped walking. What right did she have to assume the reason for his sad appearance was her? Would he even want her? She hadn't contacted him in months. She thought back to the flurry of activity that had brought her to this moment. The phone call to her father after leaving the chapel, the tears and apologies, the private plane ride he had arranged to get her to the ranch.

Her impulsive decision that had seemed so right and romantic now appeared reckless and risky. Madison closed her eyes and took a deep breath. She could do this. Silently, she prayed for strength, and put one foot in front of the other.

The wind shifted. Samson whinnied, acknowledging her presence for the first time, and Carsten turned. His gaze met hers and his expression changed.

She gave a sheepish smile and started walking faster. She couldn't read his face. The nervous flutter in her stomach quickened. Madison forced herself to keep walking, head down, eyes averted. She stopped a few feet away.

"Why are you here?" His tone was unreadable.

Her heart sank. She lifted her eyes, weakly offering all she had. "Because of you."

The corners of his mouth twitched. Was that a smile? She couldn't tell. Oh, this was agony. What if he rejected her?

Carsten adjusted the hat on his head and swung easily from the saddle. He took a tentative step toward her. Madison recognized the motion—it was the same way he approached a nervous mare.

This time, he had nothing to fear.

She crossed the distance between them with a few long strides and wrapped her arms around his neck. "I missed you."

"I missed you too." His grip tightened around her waist. "I've been waiting. Waiting and trusting."

She risked her heart with a single whisper. "I love you." The smile in his eyes made the risk worth it.

She leaned back to study his face, running a hand over the firm jaw, the slightly crooked nose, and then tucked her palm against the warmth of his neck.

He rested his cheek against her wrist and briefly closed his eyes. "I love you too, *mein angel*."

The softly spoken words sent a shiver rippling down her spine. She smiled. An angel was what had gotten her into this entire mess in the first place.

But from the love shining through Carsten's clear blue gaze, she knew in her heart that it had all been part of God's plan—to bring her to a place of love and trust that she never knew existed, with both her Heavenly Father and with the man standing in front of her.

"I have something for you." Carsten released his hold on her, and Madison reluctantly stepped out of the warmth of his embrace. She watched as he dug in the front pocket of his Wranglers.

He held out his closed fist. Madison opened her palm.

A diamond solitaire dropped into her hand.

She gasped, and tears immediately pooled in her eyes. "How did you know I would come back?"

"Faith. And a lot of prayer." Carsten slipped the ring on her left ring finger.

Madison couldn't believe it. She held up her hand. The diamond glittered in the fading sun like a flame. She felt the same fire start from her toes and begin burning up into her heart.

With a saucy grin, she lowered her hand. "There's just one problem left to solve."

Carsten raised an eyebrow.

Madison burrowed into the folds of his denim jacket, wrapping her arms around his waist. "Will we have the wedding here, or in Germany?"

"I take it your answer is yes." Carsten grinned appreciatively.

"Yes." Madison looked up into his face.

"Then I say we get married wherever your heart desires."

Madison bit her lower lip. "I want to get married at home."

"And where is your home, *mein angel*?"

"With you." She sealed the deal with another kiss.

Carsten lifted her up in his arms, and spun in a tight circle. Madison laughed, pounding her fists against his chest. "Let me go!" She shrieked.

"Never." He kissed her again.

Madison snuggled up against his chest and relaxed. For the first time, she felt at peace. She felt safe.

He pulled back slightly." I think there is someone who wants to see you."

"Oh?"

"Someone with a gray coat and messy hair."

"Unless you have a great aunt I don't know about, I'm assuming it's Sasha."

"I meant Rita, but Sasha will want to see you too, I'm sure." He dodged the punch Madison aimed at his arm.

Carsten picked up Samson's reins. "How about a ride to the house?"

She looked up into his eyes and knew she couldn't deny him anything.

His gaze grew serious. "You'll be safe with me."

"I know. I always am." She watched as Carsten mounted and reached down for her. With his help, she slid onto Samson's broad back and wrapped her arms firmly around Carsten's waist.

As they rode slowly to the ranch, she marveled

at how far she had come in the last few months. There was no limit to the goodness of God. He had taken her, molded her, and given her the gift of forgiveness. Not just for herself, but enough to pass on to her father.

Madison rested her cheek against Carsten's shoulder. The future wasn't certain. She wasn't sure where they would live, or where they would get married, or what would happen to her design business. But she knew those details would work themselves out. God had brought her this far, and He wouldn't fail her now.

She was finally home.

Epilogue

"Greta! Lukas! Get back here!" Madison laughed as her two blonde-headed children climbed onto the wall of the fountain and reached over to splash water at each other.

"You heard your mother." Carsten's firm voice did the trick, and the kids stepped carefully off the wall.

Madison grabbed each one by the hand and knelt down to their level. "Do you know what happened right here, at this very fountain?" Her tone lowered mysteriously, and both kids leaned in with eyes wide.

"This is where I met your father for the first time." Madison couldn't help but glance into Carsten's eyes at that moment, and she felt as if it were yesterday, rather than almost fifteen years ago.

The air sparked with the intensity of their gaze, and for a minute, Madison forgot where she was. A tugging of her shirtsleeve brought her back into the present.

"I wanna play in the water." Greta's eyes, blue like her dad's, were pleading. Madison laughed and swung her daughter up on her hip. "Not today. It's too cold." She tugged the child's hat down farther over her ears. "We'll come back in the summer."

"We'll come back often." Carsten promised as Lukas turned the same pout on his father.

Carsten took Lukas by the hand and wrapped his other arm around his wife. "Germany is special." His gaze caught Madison's again, and he winked. She flushed red. He laughed. It was an old routine. He never got tired of making her blush, and she loved the fact that he could do it.

"Do you think Rita is ready to watch the kids for a while back at the hotel?" Carsten whispered in her ear. A grin tugged at the corner of Madison's lips and she turned her gaze to meet her husband's. "I hope so."

As she walked back to the hotel down the streets of the foreign city, Madison couldn't help but thank God for the abundant blessings he had bestowed on her life. She took a deep breath of the fresh air and smiled at her husband and children at her side.

The clock tower chimed above them, and she closed her eyes, listening to the familiar sound. Her life was no fairytale. It was real.

And it was better.

You Can Help!

At Pelican Book Group it is our mission to entertain readers with fiction that uplifts the Gospel. It is our privilege to spend time with you awhile as you read our stories.

We believe you can help us to bring Christ into the lives of people across the globe. And you don't have to open your wallet or even leave your house!

Here are 3 simple things you can do to help us bring illuminating fiction™ to people everywhere.

If you enjoyed this book, write a positive review. Post it at online retailers and sites where readers gather. And email your review: reviews@pelicanbookgroup.com (this does give us permission to reprint your review in whole or in part.)

If you enjoyed this book, recommend it to a friend in person, at a book club or on social media.

If you have suggestions on how we can improve or expand our selection, let us know. We value your opinion. Use the contact form on our web site or e-mail us at customer@pelicanbookgroup.com

God Can Help!

Are you in need? The Almighty can do great things for you. Holy is His Name! He has mercy in every generation. He can lift up the lowly and accomplish all things. Reach out today.

Do not fear: I am with you; do not be anxious: I am your God. I will strengthen you, I will help you, I will uphold you with my victorious right hand. ~Isaiah 41:10 (NAB)

We pray daily, and we especially pray for everyone connected to Pelican Book Group—that includes you! If you have a specific need, we welcome the opportunity to pray for you. Share your needs or praise reports at http://pelink.us/pray4us

Free Book Offer

We're looking for booklovers like you to partner with us! Join our team of influencers today and receive at least one free eBook per month. Maybe more!

For more information
Visit http://pelicanbookgroup.com/booklovers